TRU

Published by:
Retreat Publications,
The Retreat,
Down Park Drive,
TAVISTOCK,
Devon, PL19 9AH

Typeset and printed by:
Antony Rowe Limited,
Bumper's Farm,
CHIPPENHAM
Wiltshire
SN14 6LH

ISBN 978–0–9538984–1–1
    0–9538984–1–5

Also by David Mudd

Cornishmen and True
The Innovators
Down Along Camborne & Redruth
The Falmouth Packets
Cornish Sea Lights
Cornwall & Scilly Peculiar
About the City
Home Along Falmouth and Penryn
Around and About the Roseland
The Cruel Cornish Sea
The Cornish Edwardians
Cornwall in Uproar
Around and About the Fal
Around and About the Smugglers' Ways
Dartmoor Reflections
The Magic of Dartmoor

Co-author

Murder in the Westcountry
Facets of Crime
Strange Stories of Cornwall
Wiltshire Mysteries
The Cornish Year Book

Crime Fiction

Let the doors be lock'd

Short Stories

Better with a Pinch of Salt

SUGAR 'n' SPICE

David Mudd

ABOUT THE AUTHOR

Writing, politics, lecturing and loving the sight of a captive audience – plus, of course, anything to do with his native Cornwall – are among the greatest pleasures of David Mudd's life.

In June 2005 he realised that the 72 years that have passed since his birth in Falmouth could neatly be divided into one third using words, one third abusing them and one third playing with them. In addition to his 22 years in politics and the same number behind pen, pencil, typewriter or microphone, he has tried a variety of short-lived jobs ranging from making choc ices to managing a tough London ballroom in the Teddy Boy era; from life afloat in the Merchant Navy to a spell with Cornwall County Council; and from running a public affairs consultancy to working with a touring theatre company.

'SUGAR 'n' SPICE' takes him to a total output of twenty-four books covering social history, crime and humour. He is a popular figure on the West Country speaking circuit and has lectured on board British and American cruise liners.

In the May 2005 general election, David stood as an independent parliamentary candidate on a 'plague on all your houses' ticket designed to make politics more open and responsive to the views of the people. Sadly the intended plague only turned out to be a minor infection and he finished mid-way down the list of nine candidates!

His wife, Diana, is a successful poet. In 2004 her first anthology, *'Diamonds, Beads and Ashes,'* was awarded a prize by an independent panel of judges. In 2005 she was listed as one of Britain's Top 100 poets in a literary publication.

ABOUT THE BOOK

Just how long *is* a short story?

There is no golden rule. In this anthology, for instance, 'short' means anything between 750 words and 4,500. Similarly, there is no rule of thumb as to what a short story should be about, or what style an author should adopt in writing it. It's a matter of literary freedom. The only thing that isn't totally free is the cost of the book. For this the author expresses his regrets: but mere apologies are insufficient to meet the bills that arrive from the printer, the bookseller and the Inland Revenue in due course.

Within this qualified air of freedom, the author has unapologetically plundered that great treasury of existing fiction to craft the changing styles he has felt best suited to set the context or content of each story.

Spike Milligan, Jane Austen, Raymond Chandler, Edgar Alan Poe and Roald Dahl have thus cast their recognisable shadows across stories of romance, lust, the chilling and the bizarre, the happy and the threatening, of death and of crime.

The author even uses his deep love and respect of matters Cornish to introduce a bunch of well-meaning cash-starved Cornish fishermen living near Land's End. They try to earn money in two traditional ways – smuggling and wrecking – before coming up to date with their hilariously planned and executed hi-jacking of a passenger liner.

DEDICATION

This book is respectfully dedicated to all those real and imaginary people whose lives, stories, inspiration and comic situations may – or may not – have contributed to each, all (or none) of the stories to be found in its pages.

For those with a wish to take matters further in any way, it is stressed that no character, event or combination of factors and events, whether real or imaginary, bears any resemblance or implied connection to any person or persons living or dead, or to any incident or occurrence that may or may not have involved them at any time.

And to my long-suffering wife, Diana – this really **_IS_** my last book!

The Stories

THE FORGER

[There is rarely any public disagreement amongst those seeking to identify the world's oldest profession. But ask a different question: 'What is the oldest skill in the world?' and there is no such unity of thought.

Given that envy is high on the list of deadly sins, then it would seem logical that the skill of the forger must claim a senior status. After all, materialism and innovation will always attract the dedication of those who are better able to copy than to conceive or create.]

Nobody had ever seriously doubted that Joseph Wendgradt would eventually go to prison.

At school his skill as a promising young forger had laid a long and distinguished trail of written deception in its wake. He wrote and signed more 'absence-through-sickness' notes on well-copied surgery notepaper in a week than the average harassed family doctor. He could massage a dismal school report into a glowing record of achievement of which parents were justly proud.

As he pointed out, he was more than successful in falsifying records that would camouflage the usual lacklustre performance of his fellow pupils.

At the age of fourteen he could churn out a prescription that would satisfy the cursory glance of a pharmacist, or bogus receipts for those who needed them to misrepresent the expenditure claims of their tax returns.

It was not merely the copying talent that he possessed through experimentation, care and diligence; in the process he also acquired a detailed knowledge of accountancy and of drugs and medications as well.

It came as some relief to Joe's parents when he announced that he was going to Amsterdam to study art. Here, they reasoned, he would be out of harm's way and in a tolerant society where, with marijuana, cannabis and heroin virtually freely available and a very liberal tax regime, there would be little call for his work – and, thus, a greatly reduced chance of his ending up on the wrong side of the law.

He attended the Amsterdam College of Art and was soon immersed in the magical world of the textures and techniques of Rubens, Van Gogh, Vermeer and Rembrandt. With breathtaking dedication he studied the stories of their lives as well as the social, sartorial and artistic influences that had inspired their work.

At the end of his third year at college he could, it was said, paint a reproduction Vermeer that would defy all but an expert... and Joe Wendgradt was fast becoming an expert.

In fact, he had become so much an authority that aficionados could not accept that a comparatively young man of twenty-three, from Golders Green, could be such a master in his own field.

He overcame this by changing the date on his birth certificate to add five years to his age and become Jos Van Haufmeister. A few more sleight-of-hand tricks with pen and official documents and his birthplace became Groningen.

To be fair to Jos, he knew his painters and their work. He was called in as an expert valuer by insurance companies, and as an unquestioned authority who could identify and date works of art. Several police agencies in Western Europe used his expertise in identifying works of art recovered after theft or disappearance.

In a way it was the insurance companies who led his thinking in the general direction his mixed talents would eventually take him and – incidentally – towards fulfilling the forecasts of all those who had predicted he would end up behind bars.

On several occasions he was asked – by collectors wishing to put a reproduction on show after the original had been stolen – to undertake a commissioned copy that would resemble the original as closely as possible.

Jos had read of, and studied, everything available regarding the skills of Henricus Van Meegeren.

Van Meegeren had been arrested by the Dutch authorities in 1945 and charged with illegally selling Dutch national art treasures to the Germans during the Nazi occupation. With anti-German feeling running high in liberated Europe at that time, Van Meegeren knew that he was facing a long period of imprisonment for his actions.

He was doubly damned as both a collaborator and a thief... or so it seemed until, virtually on the eve of his trial, he made an amazing confession. Every picture he had sold had been a forgery. Far from endangering the Dutch artistic heritage, he had protected it while – in so doing – he had cheated the German 'experts' of huge sums of money.

The very skills Jos had carefully developed from his school days were now being used, likewise, to guarantee a continuity of exhibition until such time as damaged or withdrawn originals were located, restored and replaced.

But what of those that were never found? Was there, somewhere in the world, a wealthy collector of great paintings who had his own private gallery in which the masterpieces were secretly displayed to satisfy his own indulgence in possessing great art?

It was while he was working on a replica Goya of which the original had been stolen from the Earl of Stratton's collection at Arwenack House, that he was first approached by a man he came to know as 'Deep Throat.'

'I've heard that your work is good, but can you turn mere skill into genius?' he was asked.

The caller went on: 'That missing Goya will never be recovered. It's gone to – shall we say – a "specialist" collector. Intermediaries have already offered us up to three times its market value.'

Jos interrupted: 'Just what is all this about?'

'Well, think it through. There's only one original. It will never be seen again in public but other private collectors would pay a fortune for it. If you could produce a replica of even higher quality than Van Meegeren would have achieved, the copy could then be conveniently 'recovered' by investigators after a tip-off and sold back to the insurance company dealing with Lord Stratton's loss. As the company's expert you would only have to authenticate your own work.

'With the painting recovered, the search would be called off and my clients would stand to collect some £800,000 by way of reward for "recovering" the fake. This would more than offset the total outgoings of the whole operation, including your fee.'

It was the exciting professional challenge, rather than merely the £100,000 offered, that appealed most to Jos.

'But even if I agreed to do the job, then how would the transfer arrangements could be carried out?'

'That's the easy bit. You complete the copy and deliver it to a furniture depository under an assumed name and address. You send us the receipt through an accommodation address and we collect the merchandise. That way there's no possibility you can be traced and you don't even get to know who or where your client is.'

'And how do I get my money?'

'Well, we certainly won't pay you by cheque or credit card! No, when we're satisfied with the job, we'll put the cash – in Stirling, Dollar and Euro bank notes – in another small crate, deliver them to the storage company and send you the receipt. Then, when you're ready, you call and collect.'

Despite certain misgivings, Jos decided that it was worth gambling the time and materials involved. It was exciting. If the outcome was no worse than that he would be the victim of a complex fraud, then that could be chalked up to experience. After all, his reputation wouldn't be at risk as surely nobody would claim that they had tried to entice him into forgery. Anyway, every copy he made added to his own expertise in reproduction.

His only immediate difficulty was the basic one of what to do with bundles of assorted banknotes. He could hardly pop in to his local bank with them.

The answer would be to open a deposit account in Fiji, the Bahamas or the Cayman Islands. He could book a legitimate holiday in the best possible hotel, travel first class, deposit the money and return by air. The idea appealed to him the more he thought about it.

Jos accepted the deal and was soon at work on the Goya as well as a Titian. It was, he found, weirdly uplifting and a bizarre privilege to work simultaneously on two great works of art. It was truly a rare privilege to paint in the style and the footsteps of the masters.

The delivery and payment arrangements went smoothly. There was, he thought, truth in the false belief of there being honour amongst thieves as, from a bundle of high denomination British banknotes, he paid for his flight and accommodation in Bermuda.

It was almost too good to be true. . . . His future was now assured.

As he sat in the Dock at the Old Bailey, he switched his thoughts from the sounds around him to study the historic setting of his trial.

What a picture one of the masters could capture – the centuries-old darkened panels, the massive oak tables, the wrought iron, the brass, the ornate iron scrolls. Then there was that golden shaft of light spewing down from arched windows, filling the foreground with what seemed to be a searchlight of piercing radiance while – at the same time – casting into contrasting darkness all that lay behind it. That gloomy background was, in its turn, punctuated by the vivid colours of the judge's robes, with the leather-clad law books opened at well-

5

worn pages, the glass of water, the judge's gloves neatly folded across the Bible.

How the great painters of old would have loved it.

Even Van Meegeren – he who almost sixty years earlier had been accused of stealing the very pictures he had forged – would have been amused by the irony.

Jos, had never once been even suspected of art forgery.

He pulled himself back to focussed awareness as he heard Crown Counsel utter the words that could not be denied and would lead him to prison for six years.

"My Lord, the accused stands before you charged with feloniously having in his possession, and with uttering with intent to defraud the Islington branch of BarbadAway Travel, a substantial quantity of counterfeit British £50 banknotes ... "

THE PEDANT AND LOLITA

[Words should form the essential scaffolding of clear and concise communication. To purists, therefore, the slightest error should be instantly isolated and then graded a capital offence. It is said that there is a breed of grammatical masochists who deliberately seek out and inhale the sloppy, the unclear and the ill-presented as a source of self-flagellation.]

If only Vladimir Nabokov – or even George Bernard Shaw – hadn't got there first.

Christopher Williamson-Eyre was no Professor Higgins yet there were, he reflected, certain undeniable similarities of a platonic nature between him and Kylie Smith.

He was now a crusty old teacher at a minor English public school. His Oxford MA seemed antiquated and irrelevant, he thought sadly, against the young philistines who sat before him in openly restless and rebellious rejection of his efforts to teach them English.

He attempted to impart to his pupils the gravity and beauty of the construction and use of their mother-tongue handed honourably and in trust to them by generations of scholars. Evolving man had turned guttural grunts and snarls into unambiguous words that, via the half-way point of drawings on the walls of caves, now had an inviolable clarity of meaning.

In fact, as he overheard their verbal exchanges with their ritualistic jargon, he often opined to himself that two millennia had been the tool of regression rather than progression in the communications skills of the juvenile human animal species.

At least he was not alone in his general views of the pupils.

Adele Thomas, the music teacher, was similarly disillusioned. She, however, attributed the total tonal deficit to which her lessons were subjected, to a form of self-induced deafness caused by close exposure to the outpouring of high-decibel discordant noise. This, she had been told, by her sports-teacher colleague, Damien, was seemingly known as 'pop' or 'rap' or 'heavy metal' or some such similar phenomena.

Damien was the one staff success at Passmore College. Even before that sad, sad, foolish day when the eight-hundred year college had become a state-funded co-educational establishment, he had been popular with the boy pupils. It seemed to Christopher that there was some unfathomable connection between sport and an assumed link to sexual virility and performance. It was even rumoured (according to Adele) that certain of the young ladies who now swarmed around Damien had the wildest of indescribable fantasies about what was implicitly obvious in the nether regions of his glistening, skin-tight lycra track clothing.

As had always been the case with unmarried members of staff, Christopher lived in a college apartment. It had an overcrowded and untidy bedroom, a bathroom with a metal bath stained at the plug end by years of drips from the spout of the gas geyser perched above it ... and a lounge that was more like a library.

Literary tracts and leaflets spilled from every shelf, ledge and book-case. His academic gown (thrown down in disgust in 1968 when the new head had ruled there would henceforth be girls admitted to offset the declining number of male entrants) was where he had discarded it in disillusioned, betrayed, anger that ghastly day. There were toppling piles of books, photographs, newspapers, certificates, lecture notes, and anthologies.

The fireplace exuded the indelible smell of freshly-cooked toast. This was in no way remarkable as he literally lived off incinerated bread lovingly twirled over the coal fire on the distorted and discoloured toasting fork that had accompanied him from his room at Oxford some thirty (or was it forty?) years earlier.

Not that he was set in his ways! Some afternoons his toast would be smeared with Marmite ... on others with bloater paste. Sometimes it would be thickly spread with rich dairy butter and, on others, a crumpet would replace the bread as the chosen meal.

Bread or crumpet, the degree and colour-intensity of the toasting would be fine-tuned to its preferred traditional blackened hue.

Christopher also had a cardigan. It was grey and had heavy leather buttons which, through, the passing years and the expansion of his stomach, now barely found purchase in the misshapen and enlarged holes once designed to accommodate them snugly.

It was as well-darned as any item of clothing that had survived some thirty (or was it forty?) years of uninterrupted daily service. One of the main causes of regular repairs was his pipe. Whenever he lit it, it emitted a shower of glowing embers reminiscent of a volcano in the throes of eruption. The misshapen garment would, in fact, have never been washed at all were it not for the housekeeper taking occasional furtive action on a windy or dry day, to rinse it, dry it and replace it

9

where it always hung subserviently on its hanger awaiting his return each afternoon at four-twenty-two precisely.

At four-twenty-three he would make his main social decision of the day – bloater or Marmite – select two pieces of bread, stoke the fire, impale bread on toasting fork, use a teaspoon to scoop butter out of its plastic container and settle down to what he still regarded as the BBC Home Service on his wireless.

The same thoughts crowded his tired mind at this time each afternoon. Why plastic containers for the butter – what was wrong with the old grease-proof paper wrappers? Why call a wireless a radio or a trannie? Why had they changed the name of the Home Service to BBC Radio 4? It was, he knew, all part of a plot to undermine the hallowed foundations of a civilised and literate society. His questions always compared a changing and unacceptable present with the stability of Britain's glorious and dignified past.

The evening news bulletin was a similar ordeal. News Readers (why did they not still call them announcers?) seemed to mumble their way through complex topics at a speed that would have beaten Isaac Pitman!

And as for those so-called 'presenters' . . . they were little more than self-opinionated terriers snapping and yapping mercilessly at the heels of those who deserved respect for their knowledge-based views.

More than anything else, Christopher hated what he regarded as 'the appalling diminution of grammatical skills made so demonstrably obvious in every news bulletin.'

So great an exception did he take to these that he regularly corresponded with the so-styled 'Head of News.' The fact that he rarely received even token acknowledgment merely confirmed his suspicion of the cultivation of a programmed institutional laxity towards the spoken word, he thought.

Using the cherished Parker '51 he kept for important issues, he had even written a letter of complaint to the BBC about a broadcast news item that a teenager had 'gone missing,' challenging the Corporation to conjugate the verb 'to go miss.'

He sent a copy of this missive to '*The Guardian*.' The newspaper (rather gleefully, it seemed) agreed with him.

However, he was soon writing to the BBC about 'the growing Americanism of British newspapers like '*The Guardian*.' His grievance on this occasion was that the answer to the crossword clue: 'A theatre guide? (seven letters)' utilised only seven letters as 'program' whereas the correct spelling should have been 'programme' with nine.

Indeed, he reflected sadly, too much of his time and knowledge was nowadays dedicated to the necessary duty of correcting the sloppiness and errors of others rather than allowing him time to write the novel that, he already knew, would become a modern classic.

So that was it, Christopher was a pedantic and grammatical snob... and he worked at a college where entry on potential academic merit had become of lower importance than the ability of the parent to pay what the governors delicately described as 'Prestige Money.'

It was this policy that had brought Kylie Smith to Passmore.

She was a girl, as he put it, 'of common, obvious and rather vulgar, but unusual beauty.' He even dared, in one fleeting – but hastily dismissed – unguarded moment, to recognise a scintilla of personal physical attraction towards the vivacious teenager who soon had the college at her feet.

She would, of course, marry successfully by and within the lower standards of her class, he thought.

Young ladies from the college had once been presented as debutantes, whereas Kylie's ample physical attributes – never discreetly hidden – would more likely be flagrantly exposed at discos – 'or whatever the damned things are called.'

But, and he couldn't deny it, there was something hypnotically mesmerising about the girl. 'Class?... Definitely not. Potential?... Yes, in a rather frightening and obvious way,' he thought.

Her father, euphemistically described as an 'import/export entrepreneur' was nothing more than a scrap merchant who exchanged rusty cars and refrigerators with dealers in Third World countries for textiles and cotton goods to be offloaded in bulk to certain mail order firms at a considerable profit.

'Any man who would export the destroyed to import the defective would have never dared to apply to Passmore in the good old days,' Christopher reminisced ... 'in fact, it's debatable whether or not that dreadful man can write anything other than his name,' he concluded spitefully.

Kylie was no fool. She surprised Christopher (and Adele with whom he discussed the matter) by totally rejecting the flattery and the

11

approaches of that young lothario Adonis, Damien, in his lycra suit. Indeed, she seemed to spurn every one of the lustful stage door Johnnies who managed to line the paths she trod within the campus.

Even stranger was the fact that she seemed, much to his own amazed pleasure, to wish to establish a close personal relationship with himself!

At his classes she was always the first to arrive and the last to leave. She listened intently and, although her questions showed little awareness of the substance of the lesson, at least she was persistent until she received the guidance she sought.

And – was it his imagination or was it not? – but didn't Kylie seem to lean forwards towards him as he stood in front of her, revealing more of her décolletage than was right and proper between a teenaged female pupil and an elderly male teacher?

Late one afternoon she asked an unexpected question. It was one that would pose the greatest dilemma of his life. Could she, please, possibly have an hour of his time? He considered the proposition carefully before replying: 'I'm afraid not, Kylie. My commitments are such that I just do not have an hour clear between lessons.'

Like a cobra striking, she hit home. She had scored a bull's eye on the target of his vulnerability.

'No, Sir, I don't mean in class time. Could we perhaps get together on our own one evening? I know you'll be interested in what I have in mind and it would be better if we could be in private without any interruptions.'

The beauty... the innocence... the temptation... Eve's apple... the opportunity. His mind raced. Surely there could be no harm as, although the girl might appear flighty, she certainly wasn't stupid. He made a positive decision. He would delay his toast and Marmite for precisely sixty minutes to accommodate this creature of pulchritudinous temptation.

She should call on him the following evening at five o'clock precisely.

So that he would not be able to indulge himself by thought, leave alone savour body impulses, he would ask Adele to telephone him at three unscheduled times during the hour. This would act as an effective safety valve to his emotions and to the designs on his body that he suspected this latter day Lolita so obviously harboured.

At four twenty-two, as usual, he entered his rooms. He showered, bathed in carbolic soap, dusted himself with talc, dressed and waited. He set two chairs side-by-side in front of the table before, on second thoughts, placing them on opposite sides. He had no wish to be seen as seeking to pre-empt whatever it might be that she had on her mind.

She was on time but the tight little T-shirt and the brief shorts she was wearing made him wonder if she was on her way to play tennis or, perhaps, proceeding to ice-skating. She had a thick file with her and, as if wishing to tempt him, moved one of the chairs so that they were sitting side-by-side.

Her perfume was tantalising – as was her proximity to him.

His voice became strangely thick and disjointed.

'Now, Kylie, what is the matter upon which you seek my guidance or wish to discuss?'

'My ambitions,' she said, adding to the magic of the moment, 'you see Sir, I come from what you might regard as an undesirable family background and I want to use my thoughts and experiences to write blockbusters.'

His awareness of Kylie's meteoric literary potential – and in this case he saw the word 'meteoric' in its true sense of an object making a rapid descent – was such that he winced at the very thought.

'I've been writing for some time and I'd give anything (did he detect a deep significance in ''anything''?) to get into print. I wondered if you'd read some of my short stories and give me your honest opinion.'

Here was a dilemma. If he told her the blunt truth that she was hapless, clueless and hopeless as a writer, she would pass from his life forever.

He played for time.

'It would be unfair of me to make a rushed judgment, Kylie. Perhaps you would leave your stories with me until next week and you could return then for a proper discussion after I have perused them.'

She gave him what he took to be an 'I can see where you're going' smile and said 'That'll be lovely. But could we make it about nine-thirty as I have to go to a cocktail party with Mum and Dad earlier in the evening.'

He agreed and, a week later, discarded the cardigan in favour of a slim-line shirt which strained credibility, as well as itself, across his

13

rounded stomach. A liberal spraying of 'Eastern Mysteries' aerosol dampened the worst excesses of stale smoke from his pipe. The usual 150 watt bulb had been replaced by a seductive amber one of lower power and Radio 4 had given way to Classic FM. The accommodation was tidy; a bottle of wine had been chilled and placed in a battered ice bucket. Temptingly, the door to his bedroom (in which burned a stick of incense and an aromatic lamp, was dimly lit by an even less powerful blue bulb) was carefully left slightly ajar to suggest the entrance to a harem of ancient Arabia.

There was only one stumbling-block – her wish to discuss her literary efforts.

These, he had found, were abysmally bad. She was as much a stranger to verbs and adverbs as she was to tenses and syntax. There was no format, no flow, just a scrambled mixture of words and thoughts. She could split an infinitive with the skill of a micro-surgeon. As for the spelling – well, perhaps if an eccentric publisher hell-bent on ridicule and bankruptcy were to seek someone able to write a parody in the style of '*The Young Visiters*' there might be an opening for her.

But even this avenue of opportunity would be effectively sabotaged by her graphic descriptions of eroticism and sexual depravity.

She arrived in a dress so clinging and revealing that, he thought, it was mid-way between a condom and a semi-transparent sausage skin! Lost for words, he led her to the table. She enthusiastically accepted his offer of a large glass of wine and was clearly intrigued by what might lie behind the doorway leading into the partly-revealed bedroom.

'Kylie, we have to talk seriously about this. Writing fiction is not easy: in fact, the best fiction is often based on the author's own experiences... and you do not yet have that personal experience of life.'

She was furious. 'You mustn't say that,' she stormed, 'it just isn't true. I've done, seen or experienced everything what I've written about. Anyway, I don't want a lecture on morality. I just want you to get my writing put right – you know, sort out the spelling thingies and put in the right words like. I'll be very, very grateful and I'll show it any way you like. And I do mean "any way".'

Humbert looked at his Lolita. 'Kylie, have you the faintest idea what you're saying?'

'Yes, every word.'

'Perhaps,' he thought to himself, 'this explicit garbage can be transformed. At least Kylie will call on me here from time to time and something may develop between us.'

The deal was done. Kylie would have absolute control over the theme, but he would be her editor. In exchange for what he took to be the loosely veiled offering of herself for his pleasure, he would prostitute and sacrifice every last syllable of that language he held so dear.

It became an ordeal. Tenses were wrong. Words were recklessly chosen and incorrectly applied. She suffered from a form of malapropism that created words understandable only to her. A man who was claustrophobic became 'a clostrofibe'; another character was 'a hypokhondrial' and the pilot of an aircraft, in another story, was an 'aviashunal'. Had she even heard of hyperbole, it would have been ''hypurbowly'' and each gratuitous adjective would have been misspelled.

The importance and position of an apostrophe was so beyond her grasp that Christopher thought, she might more usefully be employed by a greengrocer as a sign writer.

Yes, Kylie was doing for the English language what the Vikings had done for birth control.

Christopher had one trick up his sleeve – vital if his relationship with her was ever to move from promise to performance.

He pointed out that as the stories might upset her parents were they to lie around at home, it would be better if he corrected them on his word processor and then sent them direct to publishers under her name.

He was indignant and surprised when, despite his careful editing, the stories were invariably politely rejected and returned by publishers on the diplomatic grounds that they 'do not meet our current publishing plans.' Kylie was courteously wished greater success elsewhere.

After some eight months of seeing his cherished English language ritualistically slaughtered after enduring the torture of one thousand cuts, Christopher decided that enough was clearly enough – especially when he spotted fresh love bites and bruises on her neck and such other portions of her anatomy as were only too visible to him.

Even worse, Adele told him that it was now college gossip that Kylie was often seen coming from Damien's little matted annexe behind the gym.

There was only one way to teach this juvenile Jezebel a lesson that would hurt her deeply.

The plot was simplicity in itself. From his knowledge of trade unionism he would 'Work to Rule.' He would not edit her next effort in any way whatsoever and would leave it to the publisher to tell her that her attempts were beneath contempt and unworthy even of the word 'rubbish.'

The story reached him. The title was as tasteless and ill spelled as the rest of it.

It was called: '*Hitler, the Joozse and the Hollauwcauste.*'

It was a vile catalogue of sadistic violence and gratuitous pornography.

She sought him out a month later.

'Chris, I don't know what I can do to thank you for all what you've done for me. Name it and I'll do it ... and I do mean "do".'

She held a letter in her hand from the commissioning editor one of Britain's leading publishers.

'Hi Ky,' it began. 'Congratulations on your really, really fab piece. Hey, it's like, well, kinda cool. Thank God you've got away from all that crap grammar stuff what you used to write. Us and you is going to go places together from now on, Ky babe. Warm Regards, Tristram du Pouvery.'

Christopher's blood chilled. Tristram du Pouvery had attended Passmore ten years earlier. Even then his grammar had been beyond redemption.

Christopher used his Parker '51 once more. This time the letter, to the editor of '*The Times Literary Supplement*,' expressed his gravest concerns regarding declining standards in British literature.

THE CANVASSER

[The general election of 2005 was fought more at arm's length on the negative theories and practices of political strategists, psychologists and spin doctors than by candidates offering positive policies to the voters on a one-to-one basis.

Almost un-noticed in the unleashing of a blizzard of dirty tricks and other diversions spawned by campaign chiefs with experience from the Americas to the Antipodes, a new system of guerrilla-like political sabotage appeared on the British doorstep.]

I'm a black political canvasser with egg on my face!

Now before you get confused and accuse me of mixing my metaphors, and of blatant or political incorrectness please be patient.

Black canvassing is an American political tradition. I think I'd better rephrase that – America is still too young to have developed traditions – all they have is a series of rather nasty habits. Anyway, the dark art of black canvassing has now arrived in Britain.

The activity involves playing some of the dirtiest tricks you can imagine, in a world in which standards and behaviour start below the belt and are then dragged down still further. In a nutshell, and on the basis that there's more than one way to kill a cat, black canvassing is designed to act subversively and relentlessly against the character of whoever is defending a marginal seat at election-time.

It begins with the knowledge that defending Members of Parliament or Congressmen need to create as much blue water as possible between themselves and the official Party line if there's to be any hope of getting back. Even more important is the 'trust me, you know I'm a good guy' card.

The job of my ilk, therefore, is to use every dodge in the book to gnaw away at the personal popularity and stock of good-will that exists between the candidate and individual voters. Make an honest guy seem like a selfish, arrogant, uncouth and thoughtless person as much as you can. In that way you can, in dribs and drabs, filch away those all-important votes which, in a tightly run contest, could mean just hanging on or being chucked out.

Machiavellian? A bit of a nasty job?

Yes!

Although his name doesn't really matter as I'm talking more about the hunter than the fox, the man I've been brought in to destabilise is called Edward Johnson.

Decent name, decent guy.

I don't need any equipment for my job other than a dirty denim jacket and jeans when operating in wealthier parts of a constituency and a natty Gucci or Saville Row suit for visiting homes in the poorer ones.

Confused? It makes sense when you think about it.

Where was I? Ah, the clothes. People in the stockbroker belt generally resent scruffy tramp-like individuals calling on them. It makes the place look untidy. 'So you're from Ted Johnson,' they say pointedly. You can see that they feel that if Ted is supported by riff-raff then, perhaps, he's really not their kind of man.

At the other end of the scale, poorer people are nervous if their neighbours see a snappily-dressed man dressed like a Harrods model on their doorstep. They may think he's a detective, a tax man, or someone from the Town Hall. Either way, he's unwelcome. 'If that Ted Johnson thinks his load of toffs have anything in common with us, he'd better start looking for votes somewhere else.'

Oh, and I forgot to mention it, I need a clip-board with a pencil and electoral register for all houses, plus a huge rosette with the name and campaign colours of the person I'm trying to unseat.

The clip-board and electoral register are vital on all doorsteps. Since everyone likes the entire world to know that their home is their castle, ask them their name. The fact that the caller hasn't even taken the trouble to look it up on the printed register rankles and may cause them to change their votes away from the candidate whose canvasser is now taking up their time.

I've only a few days to complete my mission. Start too soon and you're sure to get rumbled: start too late and there isn't time to maximise the effect. Most people vote on a Thursday, so my job runs from the previous week.

By the way, the black canvasser will carry as many election addresses and other campaign material as possible – all of it clearly identifying the target figure.

Gates are amazingly useful, too, in costing votes. If they carry a sign saying 'No Canvassers,' then I violate this and march right in. Having incurred their cold fury, I then brandish the rosette under their nose and say how relieved I am that Ted is so different to the rivals. Human nature makes it inevitable that I'll be asked 'What do you mean?'

Lowering my voice to an 'I know I shouldn't really be saying this to you – but I know it'll go no further,' stage whisper, I then hint that one or more of the other candidates has a dark moral or criminal skeleton in the cupboard and keeping their fingers crossed in the hope that it won't become common knowledge until after Polling Day.

Invariably the householder is so incensed by this vicious attack that they won't vote for the re-election of someone who resorts to character assassination and Chinese whispers for self-advancement.

Oh, and talking about gates, I never close them behind me when I leave.

If the voters are out – but their dog is in – I antagonise it as much as possible. When they return and find Fido or Fifi mid-way between a heart attack and a nervous breakdown with political pamphlets on the mat, they'll soon decide who to blame!

If, on the other hand, the occupiers are at home, then I ask them what they'd like to see Ted Johnson support 'when he's re-elected.'

'Is he in favour of tougher prisons?' There's a slight problem here, I explain, as Ted's conscience tells him that prisoners are really only the victims of a tough society and he is working for more probation, Community Service orders and more social workers. Additionally, I say, he feels that prisons would benefit from less prison officers and more psychiatrists.

'Where does your man stand on education?' Simple question – simple answer. Ted feels that a more open and optional attitude should be introduced with more psychologists and a greater awareness and acceptance that a failed child is the product of failed parents.

The black canvasser anticipates every question that may be put to him as Ted's spokesman ... and convinces the voters that the candidate's views are uncompromisingly to the contrary.

I spoke, just now, of the importance of timing. That's why my personal strategy always includes two week-ends when the super-market check-outs are already reaching melt-down. I stagger to the '10 items only' express till with two full baskets of varied goods. As if oblivious to the impatience and animosity of those behind me, I mutter something to the effect that I'm one of Ted Johnson's support team and I'm urgently needed to get back on the doorstep as quickly as possible. I point out that one of the baskets belongs to someone else and that I'm only holding their place until they come back with something they've forgotten.

Of course, they never arrive and the penny soon drops that I've deliberately gone to the quickest check-out.

The goods come to a total of £32.58 but, as I slowly empty my pockets, I find I have left my credit card at home. Even worse, I only have £24.93 in cash. The furious murmurs grow as I then agonise over which items – totalling about £7.50 – I won't take after all.

By this stage I sense that votes aren't being won!

A car filled with Ted's stickers and posters left blocking the entrance to an old peoples' home for a couple of hours on the Sunday afternoon effectively puts the boot into the 'thoughtful, caring and considerate' bit of his election address.

Now it's true that many of the householders, shoppers, tenants, dog lovers, parents, social moralists and shoppers weren't going to vote for Ted in the first place and that all I've done is to strengthen their conviction against him. However, were as few as 70 voters to switch their allegiance from last time, he would stand to lose re-election by about 100 votes.

My personal target is to bring about a switch of more positive and impressive proportions. I aim to dissuade 300 at least, so that his defeat could be by as much as 500.

I must therefore use those who, if offended, will spread their disaffection widely and aggressively. I target bus and cab drivers. They are amongst the vocal opinion-formers of a modern society.

Offer an impatient bus driver a £10 note for a 60p ticket – 'sorry, mate, I haven't anything smaller. I'm working for Ted Johnson, you know,' will rapidly spread to every driver within the depot. Some dear old lady offering £5 for her £1.30 ticket will be eyed belligerently as the driver thinks 'I suppose she's one of Johnson's lot.'

As for taxi drivers – well, they're the most useful reputation saboteurs of them all. Wear your Ted Johnson rosette but don't tip them. You can, of course work anti-Johnson miracles by rubbing salt into the wound as you jump out of the cab. 'Expecting a tip? Well my tip is to vote for Ted Johnson.'

After several high-pressure days of working against him, I decided to take a look at this guy and, perhaps, to chuck a few awkward questions at him at his last political meeting of the campaign. From experience I know that such occasions are usually attended by those who have still not decided which way to vote.

He was a bit wishy-washy – but I found I preferred him to our own man.

To tell the truth, it was a mistake to see Ted in the flesh. Sort of by way of consolation I went to the polling station early next day and gave him my vote. It was nothing more than a token apology, I suppose.

And that leads me to the egg on my red face bit.

You see, Ted Johnson was re-elected day with a majority of one!

THE WRECKERS

[George Borlase lived at Gulval, in Cornwall, in the eighteenth century. He wrote to a House of Commons committee considering legislation against the tradition of wrecking ships on the Cornish coast.

'Great barbarities have been committed,' he said, 'my situation in life hath obliged me sometimes to be a spectator of things which shock humanity.'

He told the committee: ' The people who make it their business to attend these wrecks are generally tynners and, as soon as they observe a ship on the coast, they first arm themselves with sharp axes and hatchets and leave their tynnworks to follow those ships.'

After 250 years wrecking is now the subject of legend and ancient history. Or is it?]

There's a 'merican singer called Phil 'arris 'n' I do think o' 'e whenever us do go into *Th' Wreckers'* Bar down to Pentretha. This means I do think o' 'e quite often since me 'n' Curly Wemyss, Seth Crampton 'n' Jack Pender do go down there most alternative Tuesday evenin's 'cause we'm in th' quiz team.

Course, with Curly on board we'm a bit 'andicapped like for Curly isn't none too bright. In fact 'n's 'bout as useless as a extra leg in a three legged race. Still 'e does 'ave 'is uses from time to time. Thanks to 'e we do regular get th' booby prize – but what folk don't realise is that's what we'm after.

Look at it like this. There're eight teams. The bright buggers get first secon' 'n' third prizes. There's bugger all for numbers four down to seven, but there's always one o' they consolin' prizes for th' bottom team. So me 'n' Curly, Seth 'n' Jack do always get somethin' at th' end o' th' evenin' as well as a round or two o' free drinks from th' winners.

There's somethin' else, too. Folk do bet money on us comin' last. So when th' odds are good, us do bet on we not to lose. Us concentrates, comes in seventh 'n' picks up a few quid from th' punters. That's where Curly is a 'elp. 'e's got a mem'ry like a goldfish, 'as Curly – lasts all o' ten minutes. So us locks'n into th' loo with 'is trannie for 'alf a 'our before th' questions start 'n' 'e do usually remember a couple o' things on th' wireless news as'll come in useful later.

'T'were Curly as scooped our biggest winnin's ever by knowin' 'bout this Phil 'arris man.

Th' question, in so far as I c'n remember, was: 'In th' 1950s, which American singer got a surprise from what when 'e were walkin' by th' shore?'

Curly's 'and shoots up like a distress rocket.

'Phil 'arris 'n' it were from a gert big box.'

There was silence. All eyes turned to Curly. We thought th' poor daft idiot'd finally blowed 'is fuses, I can tell 'e.

'Well done, Wreckers,' says th' quizmaster. 'You're right.'

Curly was th' star o' th' evenin'. I asks 'n 'ow 'e did know.

'Simple, really,' says Curly soundin' like that there Einstein man. 'Th' batt'ries conked out in my radio so I did spend thirty minutes readin' anythin' I could find on th' walls o' th' loo. Somebody'd writ up a song by this 'ere Phil 'arris in which 'e was walkin' by th' shore when 'e seed this gert big box 'n opened it up 'n' much to 'is surprise, 'e discovered a blank blank blank right afore 'is eyes.'

Well, I must admit as to bein' truly 'mazed by it.

'N' then a idea came to I.

You see, *Th' Wreckers* bar 'as a collection o' items collected by wreckers down Pentretha cove. Bloody weird some o' they is, too. There's ropes 'n' driftwood in strange shapes, coins, buttons 'n' medals, lifejackets 'n' lifebuoys, diaries, photos, flip-flops 'n' old bottles.

Now before you do get th' wrong ideas 'bout what a wrecker is all upon, let me tell 'e that we Cornish aren't like they Devon ones. 'Tis said as 'ow they'd lure a ship onto the rocks by wavin' lights 'n' confusin' the crew as to where they was. They'd even kill survivors for th' laws o' th' sea says that a wreck isn't a wreck if there's anyone left alive from it. To be on th' safe side they folk up to Devon'd even kill cats, dogs or monkeys that escaped th wreckin'. They was real wreckers.

No, sir, we Cornish wreckers didn' cause no wrecks. Us just looks 'roun' for any cargo or bits 'n' pieces thrown up on our shores by th' good Lord.

'N fact parson Troutbeck over to th' Scillies 'ad a special prayer. 'Dear Lord, us devout persons do not pray that ships should be wrecked but merely that if, in Thy great wisdom, shipwrecks should 'ave to 'appen, then Thou would'st direct them to our shores for th' welfare 'n' benefit of these Thine 'umble people.'

'Amen to that,' I do say.

So we 'umble 'n' good people from Trethorra and Pentretha've never not wrecked in our lives. True, th' odd few crates o' brandy or gin, tobacco, cigars or cigarettes may've been salvaged from a stranded steamer 'n' offered to Zac ('s real name's Isaac) Pendragon, th' landlord o' Th' Wreckers from time to time or good timber sold to our builder 'n' undertaker, Jackie Curnow, but wreckin'? Definitely no.

You could, I s'pose, call we beachcombers or recyclers.

Like th' law 'bidin' people we are, us do even 'and th' occasional bit o' this or that into th' Receiver o' Wreck, th' Customs and Excise man responsible for sortin' out what's comed ashore.

Zac Pendragon, by th' way,'s always paid good money for th' relics 'e's accepted for display in the bar. Like with th' booze 'n' baccy 'e do always offer what 'e do consider to be a true price allowin' for the risk 'n' skill in winnin' th' goods, their 'istoric value plus, o' course, the mark-up 'e 'as to get for to be able to pay 'is income tax and VAT.

'N' that, really, is where I was goin' for to start this story... with th' item that is th' pride and joy o' 'is collection 'n' how 't'were me, Jack, Curly 'n' Seth as got it for 'im.

I blame it all on that Phil 'arris. If 'e 'adn' sung that there song, me 'n' Curly 'n' Seth and Jack'd 've been all right and th' Customs and Excise men would've left Zac well alone instead o' keepin' on 'arassin' 'im to 'and th' exhibit over to they.

After th' quiz us eventually walked up out o' Pentretha to cross th' cliff path down to Trethorra. 'T'were a wild night, black as a raven's 'eart. Th' wind moaned like a mermaid 'avin' a climax on th' rocks and, down below, us could see 'n' 'ear th' gert waves smashin' on th' rocks 'n' pullin' theirselves back for 'nother attack.

Our talk was 'bout our unexpected win. What, us wondered, was in that gert big box in th' song. What were that blank, blank blank? Curly, th' 'ero o' th' 'our, were sure it were somethin' rude. As 'e says, if 't'were just a bale o' cloth, they wouldn' 'ave needed no blanks for to say it.

If 't'were a bag o' drugs, then that man – in th' song – who buys just any ol' thing would've made a offer. And this Phil 'arris man said as 'ow you'd never get rid o' that blank blank blank no matter what you do.

It must therefore've been a curse or per'aps a skellington or th' albatross o' th' ancient mariner.

Says Jack Pender, after a moment o' thought: 'I wonder if 't'were 'is mother-in-law or even th' tax man?'

Now that I do think 'bout it, I must say in all honesty that our thinkin' was all a bit fanciful and that it were all th' more made fuddled by that we must've sunk 'bout ten pints o' best bitter each to celebrate our win.

Seth Crampton usually always do talk 'bout one item 'anged up be'ind th' bar atween th' rugby ties 'n' th' Manchester police 'elmet over th' Russian 'no entry' sign be'ind th' beer 'andles. It's a 'uge seed from a giant coconut tree from th' Maldives. When 'n's 'ad a few, Seth do swear as it's a pair o' elephant's knackers.

This time 'e were quiet as th' grave.

'What're 'e thinkin' 'bout, Seth?' Jack askd'n.

'Wreck'n'. Wonder if it do still 'appen today; all they ships which do still go straight up onto th' rocks even in good weather.'

'It's done to get th' insurance money,' says Jack. 'They gets an old rust bucket and fills 'er with cargo. They insure 'er to th' 'ilt, offload th' cargo in a cove at night, run 'er aground 'n' claim th' insurance on 'er as bein' a total wreck. I've read about it,' says 'e, as if to add authority to 'is theory.

Curly wasn't impressed. 'E were related to almost everyone in Trethorra and Pentretha. Everybody was a cousin o' some sort. At school 'e asked 'bout th' big family and was told by th' teacher, Miss Josie Rosevear, that it were somethin' to do with his mother 'avin' – or bein' – a bicycle.

Curly was certain that somethin' – either ghosts or pixies wavin' lanterns – were th' true cause o' wreckin'.'

As we talked, us passed a narrow bit in th' lane where they was diggin' up for to put in some new drainage pipes. Th' path was lit by 'alf a dozen o' they batt'ry lamps as do shine white to th' frontards 'n' red rearwards for to show who 'as priority.

Almost in but a single voice, Seth 'n' Curly says: 'Let's try it.'

'Try what?' asks I.

'A bit o' wreckin'. If us do take some o' they lights down th' cliffs 'n' wave 'em 'bout a bit, us can see if ships is curious or daft 'nough to come in 'n' take a look. They'm not in no real danger 'cause they'm got radar.'

Funny isn't it 'ow ten pints o' best bitter inspires your thinkin' 'n' fires your 'magination?

'What 'appens if somethin' do go wrong?' Jack asks. 'I don't know much about th' law, but I don't think you'm allowed to go round playin' at wreckers these days. I'm pretty sure I've read somewhere that it isn't allowed no more 'cept up to Devon.'

I was with Jack, but Seth 'n' Curly was all for goin' for it. As they did say, th' sight and sound o' th' breakers on th' rocks was enough to warn a complete idiot to lay off back out into safe waters. On top o' that, anyone on lookout would spot we a'wavin' th' lamps 'n' twig 't'were only four lads 'avin' a bit o' fun.

We was down on th' rocks a couple o' hours afore anyone took notice o' we.

'Twas a boat 'bout forty-eight feet long and 'er were actin' very suspicious. She showed no navigation lights 'n' was in complete darkness. 'Er was creepin' along th' coast, nudgin' quietly into each cove as if lookin' for somethin'. Curly thought 'er must be th' ghost o' a ship wrecked many years ago near where we was standin' and would come in an' take we away to join 'er phantom crew. I think 'e'd've runned away if someone'd offered to run with'n.

Us waved our lamps like what we'd seed 'em do in all they films down th' Trethorra Memorial 'all 'bout smugglers 'n' wreckers. 'Er came in closer 'n' closer, grey, dark, quiet and unlit.

As we swung our lanterns we twigged, too late, that some was showin' white and others was red.

On she comes until, with a sick'nin' crash, 'er 'its th' rocks full on an' do start for to take in water before capsizin' 'n'goin' down.

You've 'eard stories o' brave criminals ignorin' their own safety 'n' freedom 'n' goin' to th' rescue o' those in danger. We didn'. Us saw an inflatable bein' put out 'n' 'eard a voice say 'All accounted for,' before we fled.

First thing next mornin' we 'eard on local radio that she 'ad been lost in a unexplained incident but that nobody 'ad been 'urt.

Us went back to th' scene o' our wreck 'n' retrieved one item for Zac's collection up to Th' Wreckers. 'E said it was th' most beautiful object 'e'd ever seed 'n' it would give 'im everlastin' joy for to 'ave it.

'N' there it is to this day, proudly displayed 'n' with a spotlight on it 'n' the word 'JUSTICE' carved above it . . . a ordin'ry ship's lifebelt marked 'HER MAJESTY'S CUSTOMS & EXCISE'.

THE HIJACKERS

[It's hardly surprising if new financial hardships create a new range of challenges that can only be met and beaten by resorting to new thoughts and actions – or so the fishermen of Trethorra believed.]

There're two notable things 'bout 'Curly' Wemyss.

Th' first is that 'e isn' curly at all. In fact 'is 'ead's as bald as a Lemon Sole's arse if you'll pardon th' sayin'.

The second is that 'e's not too bright. On th' other 'and 'e's not so dim that 'e can't come up with a good idea from time to time. Th' real trick is to consider everythin' 'e do say ... an' then quickly chuck it overboard.

Seth Crampton, 'though, is a real goer. If 'e gets onto somethin' it's like tryin' for to get your finger out of a conger's teeth after its jaws've locked shut.

So there we was: Me, Curly, Seth, Johnnie Pascoe, Jack Pender 'n' Bill Thomas 'avin' a beer in th' back room of th' '*Merc & Mobile*' as we now call th' old '*Grinnin' Goat*' since they yuppies've took over with their lager, wine, sticky drinks and breezers.

When I say we was 'avin' *a* beer, I mean exactly that – no more and no less. Times is 'ard for we fishermen down Trethorra. Sometimes, when we gets back, they shout down to we from th' quay 'What've 'e caught?'

'A bigger bloody overdraft,' we respond, for it now often costs we more to put out to sea than it does to stay firmly anchored in th' men-only bar at '*Th' Merc*.'

If all six o' we do pile in and buy three pints 'tween we, they can last all th' evenin' and we c'n sit snug, 'n' chat, 'n' watch sport on th' big-screen television. Trouble is, they'm always showin' football 'n' tennis 'n' cricket whereas we lads down 'ere do prefer a bit o' rugger.

Course, in th' summer we can make a bob or two teachin' th' upcountry folk rude traditional songs which we do make up as we go 'long, or tellin' yarns o' th' Seven seas and th' mermaids like. God 'ow th' beer an' money do flow in from they idiots.

Curly drinks th' last slops o' th' best bitter 'n' 'e says 'Boys, we'm gotta make some real money.'

That were one o' 'is good ideas, highly perceptive 't'was to our needs.

' 'Ow?' Seth asked 'im.

'Dunno,' says Curly, 'but there's gotta be somethin' what us can do.'

We decided for to think it over for a few days.

Our ideas wasn't very good, really. Seth thought us should convert our boat, *Lovely Lady* into somethin' as looked like a real pirate ship and run cream tea trips round th' bay. But, as Bill Thomas said, she do stink to 'igh 'eaven like a dung 'eap in a 'eatweave.

Bill's idea were to run a few shoppin' trips over to Roscoff and pick up some duty frees – for our own use, of course. Funny thing, that, Bill's great great granddad got six months' 'ard labour for smugglin'. 'E weren't too bright. 'E were done for takin' brandy into France. Lucky they Frenchies did'n' cut 'is 'ead off with that jellotine thing.

That left me, Jack Pender 'n' Johnnie Pascoe to think somethin' up.

I were in favour o' burnin, th' bloody boat and divyin' up th' insurance money. Wouldn' be a lot, but it'd keep th' wolf from th' door and get we a clean slate 'gain at 'Th'Merc.'

Jack 'n' Johnnie thought 'bout organisin' a bank robb'ry. 'No,' says Seth, 'they'm got so much o' we's money already that it would only be like gettin' our own cash back. Knowin' our luck, we'd probably find 'twas early closing th' day we picked so's we'd even waste our petrol money goin' in.'

'I've, got a better idea' says Curly Wemyss, like a magician producin' a rabbit out o' a 'at, 'why not a 'ijack?'

There were a dead 'ush.

'Don't talk bloody rubbish,' says Jack, ''ow th' 'ell could us pinch a plane? If us did, we couldn' fly th' bugger. Cousin Jan's brother-in-law's got one o' they there 'elicopters, but I can't see as 'ow it would be no use.'

Curly smiles what 'e thinks is 'is intelligen' smile.

'Who said anythin' 'bout aeroplanes?' 'e asks, lookin' as if 'e were goin' to give birth to th' first good idea o' 'is life. 'They'm not th'only things as've been 'eld to ransom.'

'What do 'e mean?' says I.

'Well 'ow's 'bout goin' for the mail train?'

'That's bloody screwy, too,' says Seth. 'To begin with, 'ow do us get on th' train in th' first place? Don't stop nowhere from Penzance to London so even if we's on 'n, 'ow do us get off with th' cash? Anyway us 'asn't got th' money for to buy th' tickets.'

Johnnie adds 'is twopennorth o' negative thinkin'. 'If we'm goin' to do things proper we'm got to be perfessional 'n' dress proper with tights over our 'eads 'n' woolly 'ats like. Us'd look right pillocks goin' into that Ann Summers shop askin' for stockins' 'n' Milletts'd be sure for to remember we if us bought some o' they balac'lavy things. Anyway my cousin Terry do drive th' mail van to th' station and 'e'd know we 'owever well we was disguised.'

There it ended 'cept for Curly 'n' Seth sayin' as 'ow they'd look into it and report back so soon as they could.

Three weeks later we was together 'gain.

Says Seth: 'I've got some good news 'n' some bad news for 'e. I thought I'd get some advice from a top man in th' business. So I wrote to his 'ere Osama Bin Laden chap.'

'Don't be bloody daft,' says Johnnie, 'you don't 'ave 'is address.'

'I'm not stupid,' Seth says back, a bit 'urt like. 'I wrote to 'im care o' th' CIA office at th' American Embassy up London.'

'This' chimes in Curly, 'is th' bad news. We got a letter back sayin' "Not Known at This Address".'

'So if that's th' bad news, what's th' good bit?' Jack asks.

Curly do look smug like th' cat what's pinched th' cream.

'Why not 'ijack a ship?'

'Curly,' says Jack, 'you was born a bit daft 'n' I can see you'm been workin' at it ever since. What in th' livin' creation is th' point o' pinchin' a boat. Firstly we'm got one already 'n', secon', most o th' men 'round 'ere is as broke as we. Us could end up even worse off.'

Seth sighed: 'No, you prat, we do mean a real boat. Why not 'ijack a passenger liner? Th' ransom for th' ship 'n' passengers should be worth a few bob.'

I must admit as 'ow I was a bit dubious-like and asked th' first thing as comes into my 'ead.

'What passenger liner do 'e 'ave in mind?'

'Well', says Curly, 'I'm all for goin' for that there new *Queen Mary*. 'Er'll be full o' moneyed folk and, as 'er cost Cunard 'bout £500 million for to build, th' ransom's goin' to be pretty good.'

Jack is sensible as always. 'No, 'er'll be jam packed with radar and us wouldn' get near she without th' alarms goin' off. On top o' that,

34

there'll be security men. I've 'eard it said that 'er's protected by the Mafia and us don' wanta tangle up with they.'

Curly may be a few pence short o' a pound – like th' lift don' go right up to th' top floor with'm – but 'e can read. We sent 'im into one o' th' travel agents for to get some o' they catalogues what th' cruise people do give away.

We was really attracted to th' big ships as a kind o' win-win insurance. As Bill Thomas said, even if th' job failed and we was caught we'd be able to sell our story to th' newspapers 'n' even to 'ollywood after us come'd out o' gaol.

Bill remembered somethin' what 'e'd got on a piece of paper out o' a Christmas cracker once: 'Think BIG, do BIG and you are BIG.' It some'ow seemed to fit 'is thinkin'.

Jack Pender seed it a bit different. 'E were goin' for th' real big money, not a fall-back if it went wrong on we.

'Look at it like at this. There's only six o' we – five if Curly's mother won't let 'n come 'long. There's no way us can take a big ship 'n' its crew by surprise. I think us should go for somethin' littler,' 'e says.

Johnnie Pascoe agrees. 'Typical o' that negative blighter,' thinks Seth as 'n remembers somethin' in another cracker: 'Think LITTLE do LITTLE and you'll stay LITTLE.'

Bill, Johnnie, Jack and me gets th' majority over Seth 'n' Curly 'n' we decides on a small liner for the job. 'Er's called *Pacifico del Mar* an', accordin' to th' pictures in th' catalogue 'er's ideal.

Firstly, 'er only do 'ave a crew of 40 and they'm all foreigners. Secon', 'er only carries 100 passengers – easy to round-up. Thirdly, th' bridge 'n' crew quarters is all set well for'ard leavin' an open deck aft where us can land from a 'elicopter in th' darkness without bein' seen.

We spent th' next three weeks watchin' all th' videos 'n' telly documentaries us could get 'bout 'ijackin's. We looked at pictures o' *Pacifico del Mar* 'n' worked out where to put explosives.

As Bill Thomas did see it, us didn' need for to actually 'ave no explosives. If one o' th' officers saw a sack marked 'amonium nitrate fertiliser' at th' end o' a cable from a det'nator box 'e wouldn' call our bluff. Us could get a real box an' a couple o' crates marked 'Explosives – Keep Clear' from th' council tip beside the quarry. As for th' ammonium nitrate bags, well they'm blowin' around most farmyards.

Us went into strict trainin'. Us tied ropes round th' branches o' a 'igh oak tree for to learn 'ow to shin down 'em fast like what they Marines do when they slide out o' choppers. Then, after 'ittin' th' ground, th' first job was to plant our six sacks where they'd do damage if they 'ad real explosives in 'em and was set off.

Us timed we doin' all this 'n' then played out at gettin' th' crew captive. Seth do speak a bit o' Eyetalian 'n' 'twould be 'is job for to tell th' officers that we'd taken th' ship 'n' that we'd kill crew and passengers one by one if they did'n' surrender. Curly'd take one o' th' officers along for to show'n where us'd placed th' explosives.

Th' chief steward would 'ave to get th' passengers out o' bed as if it were a boat drill an' get them to th' cinema. By then, Seth would've got th' crew down there as well so everybody'd be accounted for and locked in.

Jack Pender's job, th' most important of all, would be to negotiate for our cash 'n' a safe escape.

We waited for th' night that *Pacifico del Mar* would be sailing near th' coast. This was so that if anythin' did go arse over tip, us could take a lifeboat 'n' get th' 'ell out o' it.

At first, only one thing went wrong. It were foggy and Cousin Jan's brother-in-law 'adn't never flown in th' foggy dark before. However, 'n' told us as 'ow 'is global positioning gear 'n' infra red things'd identify th' ship 'n' pinpoint our landin' spot fair 'n' square.

'E were bang on. 'E pointed down 'n' there, in th' dense fog she were. 'Twere th' thickest fog I've ever seed. You couldn' see but a inch in front o' 'e Us slid down they ropes, planted our bags 'n' took th' liner just like us'd prepared.

Now 'twas Jack's bit. 'E picked up th' microphone on th' VHF, tunes to channel one-six 'n' says: 'Coastguard, Coastguard, Coastguard, this is *Pacifico del Mar*. Do you read me?

'Yes, *Pacifico del Mar*, please retune to channel eight'. 'E did.

'Coastguard, Coastguard, Coastguard, listen closely as I'm not goin' for to repeat this. This is th' actin' master of *Pacifico del Mar*. We've captured th' ship 'n' placed explosives. Nobody 'as been 'urt yet but unless we receive £3,000,000 there will be casualties.'

I were a bit worried by th' response: 'What th' 'ell are you bloody playin' at, Jackie Pender? I do know your voice well enough – I've 'eard it 'nough times,' th' coastguard said.

I broke in : 'Now look 'e 'ere. This isn' for fun. Us've got th' ship 'n' its crew 'n' if us isn't sent th' money in a 'elicopter within one hour to take we off 'n' give we political immunisation from arrest, th' lot goes down. Talk to th' owners pronto,' I did say positive like.

For 50 minutes there was silence. Then comes a message in a firm voice over the radio.

'*Pacifico del Mar*, this is British warship *Pursuit*. I am supported by other units and have orders to take extreme measures, if necessary, to recover the ship. Consider your position.'

Five minutes later: 'Warship *Pursuit* to *Pacifico del Mar*. This is your last chance to give yourselves up. We are one mile from your position. I have been joined by an SAS hostage release unit and they have been instructed to re-occupy you. The operation will commence in exactly four minutes.'

'Shit', I thinks to myself. 'What th' 'ell do I do now?'

Two minutes to go. Chance for me to try one final bluff for to at least win a bit o' thinkin' time.

'*Pacifico del Mar* to *Pursuit*. If so much as one o' your boys lands on this 'ere deck, I'm openin' th' sea cocks 'n' us'll send th' whole bloody lot down to Davy Jones' locker ... 'n' that's no idle threat.'

'Warship *Pursuit* to *Pacifico del Mar*. That option is not open to you. You are in dry dock.'

THE SMUGGLERS

[To the old (and not so old) Cornishman, smuggling has always been a religion and a moral duty as well as a useful generator of cash. Those involved in the many links in the chain were, after all, merely carrying out a venture that had commendable Anglo-French entrepreneurial motives as well as giving employment to those working for the law enforcement agencies and providing the Royal Navy (albeit unwillingly) with some of its finest seamen.

Even the strictures of John Wesley could not put an end to the trade. His rebukes merely hit the half-way house of making some smugglers feel a little guilty – none more so than some of the fishermen of Trethorra.]

You'm prob'ly not noticed this, but I'm not what you'd call a educated man.

Miss Josie Rosevear, down to Trethorra volunt'ry boys' school once said as 'ow I were beyond educatin' 'n' ought to be put to work so soon as possible. 'Er did'n' even rate too 'igh my best mates, Curly Wemyss 'n' Seth Crampton 'n' said as 'ow we was unteachable 'n' didn' not concentrate on nothin'. Th' trouble was, she did say, that we'm all dreamers 'n' always miles away from where us should be.

Yes, us weren't too good at bookwork, but us know'd more'n Josie 'bout winds 'n' tides 'n' currents 'n' where th' mackerel 'n' pilchards do run. Us did know 'ow to mend nets 'n' 'ow ropes do best be coiled.

Th' other day I was reminded o' somethin' 'er once did say.

I think Josie were talkin' 'bout philosophisers or old teachers or somethin'. My mem'ry ain't too great, but I think 'er was on 'bout some Roman or German chap called Eucalyptus. 'E 'n' 'nother thinker called Piethagrias 'ad a belief that 'ist'ry do come roun' full circle in th' fullness o' time.

Didn' really take it on board at th' time. I were worryin' 'bout apples droppin' off trees into someone's boilin' kettle or some other science yarn 'er were tellin' we.

Anyway, week las' Tuesday I were rummagin' round in th' loft o' th' cottage 'n' I comed across th' family Bible. I were staggered for to find my name were in there 'n' my cousins at th' time included a Curly Wemyss 'n' a Seth Crampton. I 'ad a bit o' trouble readin' it so I pops alon' for to see Johnnie Pascoe. 'E's good with readin' things.

Blow me down, Johnnie do 'ave all the parish registers 'n' reports for Trethorra in th' middle 1700s as it do seem that 'is ancestry was clerks to th' chapel, to th' magistrates and to th' authorities.

Well, talk 'bout 'ist'ry comin' round; a Zac Pendragon were runnin' the pub in they days, 'n' there were a Jack Pender 'n' a Bill Thomas too.

All o' we, me, Curly, Seth, Johnnnie Pascoe, Bill Thomas 'n' Zac Pendragon'd all lived in Trethorra at th' same time at least once before. So Eucalyptus were right in 'is theories 'bout 'ist'ry comin' full circle.

Johnnie Pascoe were well read. 'E'd made it from the volunt'ry boys' school to th' grammar school and'n knew a lot 'bout th' past.

'Times were differen' then', 'e told I. 'Chances are that 'e wouldn've made it to your thirtieth birthday.

'There'd've been cholera 'n' typhoid. If 'e'd worked down th' tin mines, th' damp would've got into your chest 'n' lungs 'n' you'd be dead afore you knew you was even sick.

At sea there would've been dangers for th' fishermen. There was no social security or dole mony 'n' there was always th' chance o' bein' picked up by th' Navy press-gang and whisked off, for who knows 'ow long, in a warship 'eadin' for wars with th' Frenchies, th' Spaniards or they 'mericans.'

Service in th' Navy meant poor pay, floggins 'n' th' likely loss o' a arm or two or a couple o' legs, 'e told I.

Not a very good life, I agreed.

'N' there were worse to come.

'There was this 'ere man John Wesley goin' through Cornwall tryin' for to save souls from 'ell. 'E didn' just do it once. 'E comed back year after year to see 'ow things was goin' on,' Johnnie Pascoe said 's if 'e knawed it all off by 'eart.

This John Wesley man ('e looked just like th' fellow on they old puffed wheat and porridge boxes, Johnnie Pascoe said) comed to Trethorra in July 1753.

'My ancestor, Johnnie Pascoe, wrote down in 'is big book o' parish records that Mister Wesley preached o' th' evils o' tryin' to make a few bob on th' side by smugglin'. It seems as 'e did write in 'is diary that night: "I found an accursed thing. Well nigh one and all in Cornwall bought or sold uncustomed goods. I told them plain, either they must put this abomination away, or they would see my

41

face no more. They severally promised to do so. So I trust the plague is stayed.''.'

I could see it all, so plain as th' Bishop's Rock light. Me 'n' Curly 'n' Seth Crampton 'n' Jack Pender 'n' Johnnie Pascoe 'n' Bill Thomas was all descended from smugglers.

I travelled back, in time, to th' Wesleyman's days down 'ere.

'T'were Curly's idea. 'E were even known then as 'Curly' as 'e worked as a barber surgeon 'n' wig-maker to th' gentry – sort o' 'avin' th' ear o' th' nobility, so to speak.

Just like Curly now, 'e weren't none too bright, it do seem. The records said as 'ow 'e were two mackerel short o' a dozen. Seems that were why 'e were a barber. Saved'n 'avin' for to make up conversation 'imself. 'E listened to what customers was sayin' 'n' then passed it on as 'is own thoughts.

Curly were list'nin' to some o' they talkin' 'bout smugglin' one day.

'E were 'mazed for to 'ear as 'ow a ordinary man in a crew could make so much as £30 a night. Even Curly did know that a fisherman might only earn so much as £50 in a good year.

The three men was goin' on 'bout Mister Wesley's next visit.

'He's bound to ask us about the effectiveness of our smuggling countermeasures' said one 'and I'm afraid it's a losing battle. The more we try to stop these damned locals, the worse it seems to get'. The speaker, a stocky man with a weather-beaten face, was Captain James Belcher-Windrush, of His Majesty's Coastguard.

Lowering his voice, as if in confidentiality, he admitted: 'The trouble is that their awareness of what we are doing is much greater than what we ever know of them. In fact, several of our men come from fishing families and we're pretty confident that they tip the blighters off.'

The second man, tall, lean and young, looked every inch a soldier. The appearance was hardly surprising as he was Lieutenant Jeremy Fawcett-Twytt of the Royal Dragoon Guards.

'Yes', he agreed. 'We often surprise groups of them unloading on the shore but they scatter into the sand dunes or split up and run off along the cliffs. They hide the goods in the most unlikely of places and I'm dreading having to tell Wesley that one lot actually hid alcohol along the dip where two sections of the church roof meet.'

The third man, Captain James Fairhaul of His Majesty's Customs and Excise, was even more frustrated.

'The law actually works in their favour' he said with obvious frustration. 'Although smuggling is a serious offence, the maximum punishment is only six months at hard labour. Pretty trivial when you look at the low risk and the high reward. Even more ridiculous is that once the goods have been landed, they can then be legally and openly sold in any pub or shop that'll take them.'

Curly's ears did prick up at this 'n' it seems 'e' couldn' wait for to get me, Jack Pender, Bill Thomas, Seth Crampton 'n' Johnnie Pascoe into th' bar at Th' Wreckers for to chat with Zac Pendragon th' lan'lord.

Zac were enthusiastical for to say th' least. 'E didn' like Excise, Customs and Coastguard men at th' best o' times, always pokin' pryin' 'n' list'nin'. As for they Dragoons, well they'd come in stinkin' o' sweaty 'orses 'n' grab the best seats next to th' fire 'n' spend th' whole night over one glass o' ale. Yes 'e'd give smugglin' a go with great pleasure.

Anythin' that 'ad no risk, no questions asked 'n' a good safe profit was right up 'is street.

So it wouldn' be no difficult job for to get rid o' the goods, us decided. Th' real snag would be in settin' up what they did call a 'chain' from France to Trethorra.

Us asked Johnnie Pascoe for to look into it.

'Well,' says 'e when 'e's looked at 'is books, 'us do need a Mister Big to put up th' cash; a boat for to bring th' goods over; 'n' some pack mules for to carry th' tubs up from th' beach.

As always, Curly Wemyss do but in. 'We'm got a Mister Big. Joe Garvey, th' blacksmith, 'e's, as big as they do come.'

'Curly, you'm as thick as they do come,' I said. 'When Johnnie says 'bout a Mister Big, 'e don' mean a big man. 'E' do mean a man big with money for to put up front to pay they Frenchies for th' goods.'

But Curly were in full flood.

'Us can't use no mules, for if th' Coastguard do see we with'm they'll guess we'm smuggling. No, us mustn' use no mules.'

I were 'bout to give'n a pat on th' back for not always bein' daft, when 'e added that 'is cousin over Zennor way 'ad three ol' pet donkeys so us could use they instead. Regardin' th' boat, well us 'ad our own fishin' smack, *Lovely Lady*, why couldn' us use she?

'Because,' I told 'n, 'every Customs 'n' Exciseman man from th' Scillies to Th' Dodman knows 'er. She'd soon be recognised.'

'Not if us painted 'er in different colours,' Jack Pender said. 'What if us painted 'er red 'n' blue on one side, 'n' yellow 'n' grey on th' other. That'd confuse 'em.'

'Couldn' do that, I'm colour blind and might get on th' wrong boat,' Curly said.

There are times with Curly that I wish 'is mother'd kept th' stork 'n' let Curly fly off in th' little basket when 'e was born. Small wonder that th' parish records didn' name 'is father. Who'd want to own up to 'avin' a son like 'im?

Johnnie was still waitin' for to finish 'is say.

'We'm also goin' to need a largish team o' men on th' beach for to 'elp get the stuff 'away quickly; somewhere for to 'ide it; 'n' a intelligence man who'll find out where th' enemy are any night we're doin' a run.'

Curly were gettin' more stupid by th' minute. 'No problem with th' team. Us can get th' chapel choir down 'n' pretend they'm gettin' 'ymns ready for when Mister Wesley do come to preach to we again.

'Daft bugger,' I heard Bill Thomas mutter. 'Who ever 'eard of a chapel choir 'oldin' a rehearsal on a empty beach, in thick drizzle, at dead o' night?'

I don' know, but I got th' feeling that 'ad there been a vote on killin' Curly there and then, th' only argument would've been 'bout who should do it 'n' 'ow.

It took a few weeks to get things movin'. Zac Pendragon'd already worked out that if – as perfec'ly legal – 'e could get a reputation for sellin' good smuggled French brandy, then 'e could fill all th' kegs with inferior British stuff and sell it at four times the price without anyone spottin' the diff'rence.

Studyin' th' for sale posters at th' Custom House, Johnnie Pascoe spotted a suitable boat for we. She should've been broke up after being intercepted on a run, but Captain Fairhaul's men weren't 'gainst a bit o' private enterprise themselves 'n', after repainting 'er 'n' changin' 'er name, put 'er up for sale with no questions asked. She were black with a broad white band 'roun' 'er so even Curly couldn' mistake 'er when we reversed 'er paintwork. Us changed 'er sails from white to dark red so's they wouldn' show up in th' dark. Th' size o' she were right, too. Th' night they'd seized 'er she were carryin' nigh on ten dozen casks o' brandy, rum 'an' gin, tea, tobacco, silk, snuff 'n' playin' cards worth in all over £3,000.

I 'ad to admit, th' authorities'd done a great job in trappin' 'er. One o' th Coastguards'd flashed 'is bullseye lamp out to she with a signal they was expectin'. Crunch, 'er 'it the shingle 'n' stuck fast on th' fallin' tide. Excisemen, Coastguards,Customs, troops, wreckers and villagers joined in so almighty a binge that th' evidence was all drunk down before the Revenue men was able to get anything seized 'n' listed for to be destroyed.

Us tried a few practice runs. Lucky us did, 'cause Curly wrecked everythin' us tried.

It were 'is job to get everythin' over th' side if a possible Excise boat appeared. But 'e were always one jump be'ind. Snuff 'n silks floated away, th' sea makin' 'em useless when he throwed them over the side. Tell 'n to sink kegs o' wine or spirits 'n' 'e'd forget for to put marker floats on. Mister Wesley was 'gainst gamblin', so Curly wouldn' 'andle no playin' cards or tobacco.

Yet it were Curly who saved th' day once. Us 'ad a load o' casks for to 'ide. Seth Crampton'd arranged for 'em to go down to th' chapel vestry. Curly said as 'ow Mister Wesley wouldn't like th' chapel to be used like that but 'e prob'bly wouldn' mind if we took them up th' church and hid 'em there instead and then th' vicar'd get th' blame.

Someone'd informed on we and just as us stowed th' last o' th' stuff in th' church belfry, Lieutenant Fawcett-Twytt, armed with a warrant signed by Squire Godolphin, galloped past with 'is troop of Dragoons on 'is way to th' chapel. You can't trust no one in th' smugglin' trade. Th' squire was one o' our best customers 'n' even 'eld shares in our boat.

Funny, really, I think us'd all 'ad 'nough by then 'n' we decided on one last run.

Us cleared Roscoff late in th' evenin', ready to make Trethorra just before first light. As us set off, Johnnie Pascoe see'd a small smack overtake we 'n' set sail on a similar course. A couple o' hours later, us found out that 'er'd 'ad agents on board 'n' that they was on their way to rendezvous with th' Excise cutter, *Wideawake* 'n' to get we caught red 'anded like.

45

As us was 'bout twelve mile out from home, we was signalled 'n' asked to prepare to receive a injured seaman from a cutter calling herself *Whichever*. Under th' rules o' th' sea, us gave way 'n' as we did go to th' side to help th' man on board, we was taken unawares by Captain Fairhaul and some o' Fawcett-Twytt's men.

This was it. There was only one penalty – a stiffish six months o' 'ard labour on the treadmill at Bodmin prison followed by th' inevitability o' bein' taken by th' Navy Press gang at th' prison gates when we was let out.

Curly rose to th' occasion. Goin' unnoticed to *Wideawake's* side, 'e threw 'is 'at into th' sea 'n' shouted 'Man overboard!'

As everyone dashed to th' side to see what were goin' on, I grabbed my chance and jumped over th' rail 'n' went deep down under on th' other side under th' cutter's keel.

I remembered too late that I couldn' swim!

I don' know 'bout a drownin' man's life passin' before 'is eyes, but I knew I wouldn' survive short o' a miracle.

Then, through the bubbles 'n' the struggles; through my panic; through my ag'nies, I see'd th' face 'n' 'eard th' voice o' my teacher, Josie Rosevear. 'Er were callin' my name.

'Wake up, you idle boy. I don' know what you'm dreamin' 'bout, but my class isn' no place meant for you to sleep in.'

THE CRIME

[A juicy corpse, a femme fatale or two plus a quick-thinking ex-policeman turned private investigator are the basic ingredients of a string of stories from such writers as Raymond Chandler or even Agatha Christie.
Neither Chandler nor Christie wrote this short yarn.]

As a private investigator I'm used to seeing victims – usually toe-tagged in the city morgue if the harbour crabs ain't gotten to them first. But this guy was the worst I'd ever seen, weeping and trussed up in the psycho ward like a Thanksgiving turkey.

He was the victim of a crime that rocked the corporate institutions of Wall Street and the eateries of Manhattan to the very core. Whoever did it threatened the reputations of six major corporations in a city where greed has always reigned supreme more as a religion or a duty than a relaxation.

I went to the crime scene – Saturnino's – in a stretched limo with black windows, loaned to me by some Italian mobsters who owed me some favours. It was a good passport – the doorman didn't look for a tip from guys who travelled in vehicles like that! Neither would he ever challenge their identity as they went in bunched like footballers going for touchdown, their eyes protected by smoked-glass Polaroid shades from the non-existent glare of the equally invisible polluted New York sun.

Saturnino's is a shrine to the sensual, a mecca for the self-indulgent. Whatever you want is ready and waiting. To set the scene, the after-shave in the washroom is too pricey even for Tiffany's to stock. The seductive smells of perfume mingle with those of cigars. Mink rubs shoulders with Kashmir on the garment hooks in the check-ins.

To leave your coat there costs a fee plus an expected tip that feels like it's one week's rental of a penthouse in Manhattan. It's said that one hat check girl who used to work there, Rosa Martinez, now owns an apartment block for Latinos in the Bronx as well as a clip joint off Times Square.

It's not so much that the food sounds exotic and special. It's pretty good, I'll give you, but much of it is bought in – at a bulk discounted price – from the oriental and European eateries just down the street and, after the 'extras' of a few twirls of anorexic pea pods, carrot shavings and a sprinkling of chopped calabrese and burned tomatoes, a shot of liquidised garlic and a wedge of lemon recycled from the bar have been added, is then sold at a seven hundred per cent mark-up to diners who are usually too drunk to see, let alone taste what's on the plate.

It is, I reflected, a paradise for any would-be poisoner. In the gloom you could slip anything onto a plate or into a glass without anyone noticing.

Being wealthy enough to be accepted as a diner at Saturnino's is what it's all about. Get known there and – boy, you've arrived amongst those who make Wall Street move and shake.

And as for the tab, well the beauty of subdued candlelight ain't just that nobody can spot who's dining with who, but it's so that the punters can't read the figures on the tab too easy. Saturnino's could sell decaying coyote straight from the street, or garbage direct from the trash cans of the West side and nobody'd complain so long as the noughts on the tab stretched half way to the moon, if you know what I mean.

There's another attraction (well known to the guys down at Narcotics). That white powder in a bowl they'll bring you if you ask … well, it ain't going to be sugar or salt! Even to a rookie cop, there's something weird about the speed – hey, that's pretty near the right word – the speed they empty the ash trays between drags.

Nova Lopez is a cigarette girl who works from there – and I do mean **from** – there. She looks like she's $1,000 but, I later found out, she never tricks for less than three grand. What a chick. There must be all of nineteen inches between the top of her dress and the bottom … and you can sure see what holds it up.

Nova paid five grand for her job – but that's not unusual in high-tipping places where the hat-check girls, the cigarette girls, the flower girls and the doormen invest in buying the job and then live comfortably off the tips. I've always wondered where a doll like Nova came up with so much cash in the first place. Must be the richest profession as well as the oldest.

I told her I was investigating my worst-ever case and that it would stay my worst-ever until the next one came along. I asked her who was eating at table 7 on the night of the crime when Giovanni Lascuto had ended up in a straight jacket.

It was, she agreed (but then Nova always agrees to anything once she's pocketed the greenbacks) the worst criminal violation I'd ever come across. Nova has a photographic mind – one that's always positive and never negative except when the offer's too low.

'Let me get it right, captain,' she says.

(This is not the right time to remind her that I'm no longer in the New York police department).

'Sorry,' she interrupts and corrects herself, 'I'd forgotten that you're a PI these days. Shame about that raid you organised in 47th precinct and gotten the commissioner snorting coke with a group of hookers and weirdo junkies. Being busted can't be fun.

'Answering your question, there was Nicky Cohen, Phil Palowski, Jacko Giuliani, Pat Finnigan, Mary Buttermilk and Costos Kristos all together on table 7. I can picture it now.'

'Mary Buttermilk?' I asked, quickly spotting that she was the one person in the group who wasn't male.

Nova cut in on my thoughts. 'No, it ain't Mary you're after. She's always OK.'

OK for what? I wondered. One broad, five executives... wasn't this really something I should pass on to Lieutenant Harrigan at vice?

'When I say Mary's OK, I mean she's straight. No, not exactly straight straight if you get my meaning. She's straight to her sexuality. No nonsense with her. She's the straightest dyke in the business. She don't let males treat her, so she don't have to treat males, if you see what I mean. Us girls have a joke about her. We call Mary the astro-travel challenge.'

'Huh?' I reacted.

'Well, those rocket guys can put a man on the moon, but there's no way they're ever gonna put a man on Mary.'

She went on: 'Anyway, whoever it was who done it to Giovanni Lascuto – or didn't do it to him as the case may be – it weren't Mary Buttermilk.'

I could see that Nova wasn't hiding anything. In that dress there wasn't even enough spare space for a tiny bug to lurk without creating an obvious and visible extra bulge.

Armed with Nova's information I did what the real professionals like Poirot, Maigret, Ironside or Marlow would do. I staged a reconstruction.

I tried to confuse them like Columbo would. Before I'd even asked one question, I'd make like as if I was leaving the room and then, turning, say 'Just one more small thing.'

Funny, that trick's never worked for me.

Like Poirot does, I reseated them exactly where Nova said they'd sat that night. I asked them to remember what they'd eaten.

So far, so good.

Now the key question. Who had paid, how, and for who?

This is always difficult to unravel when you get a bunch of freeloading top executives using corporate accounts to entertain each other.

Nobody could remember who they'd paid for or how they'd paid. Even worse, each of them had at least five platinum plastic cards. Sometimes I wonder if the whole Federal budget isn't more likely to be at risk from plastic meltdown than through terrorists getting into Fort Knox.

That's something really important these global warming guys should be thinking about.

I had one last key witness, the manager, Franco Salvetti. I didn't need to use the dummy judiciary witness subpoena I always carry with me for use in emergencies. The seriousness of the crime got him to get out the tabs as soon as I asked for them.

Giuliani had paid for Kristos and Cohen on his company's American Express.

Mary had gone Dutch on Visa.

Finnigan had used his corporation's Diner's card.

That left Palowski unaccounted for.

With the experience of a lifetime I instinctively knew that he was the person responsible for the crime that had put Giovanni Lascuto into acute terminal psycho trauma.

A quick look at the charge dockets proved I was right.

As the other five distanced themselves from him, like subway passengers shunning a drunk or an evangelist having a rant on a sidewalk pitch, I swung round to face Palowski: 'I'm turning you in for severe mental assault. You paid in cash and you didn't leave Lascuto a tip.'

THE NEGOTIATOR

[The ocean bed of British industrial relations is littered with the scattered white skeletons and decomposing bodies of failed negotiators. Be they representatives of the employers or the work force, their power and credibility evaporated the moment they made their first bargaining mistake.

In the ruthless world of reaching and signing binding agreements, even the first misjudgement of the integrity and honesty of the opposing side is one miscalculation too many.]

Although people don't realise it, there are some things that happen more frequently in fact than in fiction.

That book, for instance, that always mysteriously opens on a critical page... it really does happen, as Jack Huggins was reminded while he was carrying out the annual cull of his crammed and untidy bookshelves. Some ninety per cent of the volumes would never be needed again yet, once a year, they were taken down, dusted and replaced. He would try to get round to reading them one day. Other books had memories of his previous work or carried nostalgic links to the persons or circumstances under which he had acquired them. A few, he recognised with guilt, belonged to libraries and now carried such massive overdue penalties that it was preferable to forget them than admit to his protracted illegal ownership and face the accumulated punitive fines they now carried.

He mightn't have paid much attention to the slim, blue-jacketed, copy of '*The Scots Word Book*' had it not been for the 'Thank You' card that dropped from it as he dusted it ready to return it to its usual place between '*The Concise English Dictionary*' and '*Arthur Scargill – god not man.*'

The card, from his sister-in-law Margot, was inscribed in green ink 'With grateful thanks for all your help and support without which I wouldn't have been able to get through that ordeal at Dufftown. Hope you enjoy the wee book.'

He shuddered at the memory of that cold, snowy afternoon in the heart of Scotland's Grampian Mountains. It still haunted him in a series of dramatic and disturbing nightmares.

Jack was a born political activist. His great grandfather had led the strike of the Bryant and May's matchmakers. He smiled at the irony linking matchmakers to a strike. It was, he thought, as logical as the modern sanction of 'working to rule' which meant, in effect, not working at all.

Although his father had no connection with the north-east or with shipbuilding, he had been one of the 'associates' who had marched from Jarrow to London in an act of political and trade union comradeship and solidarity.

While other classmates revelled in history extolling Britain's example and achievements as ruler of a great empire, Jack found an affinity with the Tolpuddle Martyrs, the Luddites and the trade union and Labour movements. He saw capitalism as the tool of the minority used to exploit the working classes. There were no public benefactors – merely frightened bosses who used some of their vast profits as conscience money to buy peace from those they used as subservient slaves in their dedicated task of amassing still more wealth.

Nothing could shake him from his belief of the existence of a divided society in which the oppressed workers represented integrity, graft and solidarity against the self-indulgence, greed, exploitation and corruption of the employers.

In 1945 the grammar school he attended allowed pupil Conservative, Labour, Liberal and Independent candidates to take part in a mock general election. The headmaster drew the line at Jack's desire to stand under the Communist banner. For the first-time ever, he showed his negotiating skills and argued that, if democracy was inescapably linked to the expressed will of the people, then by definition, the Conservatives, Labour and the Liberals only represented self-interest areas of political and economic philosophy. It must therefore follow that, as none of the major parties could mathematically win the overall moral support of all those casting their votes, their very existence was undemocratic.

As a consequence, he argued, it was vital to have a 'People's Party' to harness the votes of those who placed the importance of people above that of party politics.

On a manifesto that would have identified Karl Marx as a moderate liberal, and in a series of speeches displaying oratory that would have been envied by William Shakespeare and Laurence Olivier, Jack proved both points in that he took more than eighty per cent of the votes cast by his schoolmates when he stood for 'The People.'

He followed Clement Atlee's 1945 Labour government with great interest, being supportive of everything it did in the field of economic, social and industrial reform. By 1949, 'though, his support was wavering as Britain refused to disarm and was, it seemed, moving more towards the American policies on Russia and China.

In 1950 he bounced, briefly, into the Communist Party of Great Britain and three years later, after a spell of intensive training, became a young trade union shop steward at one of Britain's major car factories.

Finding the Communists to be 'too bloody establishment and predictable by half,' Jack Huggins then joined the Socialist Workers' Party.

His skills at negotiation lay in that he was light years beyond the old cart horse mentality of fellow trades unionists. As a shop steward he carefully plotted a planned strategy of advance like a general on the eve of battle. He knew what his members were demanding – and shrewdly anticipated just how far the employers would go to meet those demands.

He worked to the golden rule that, if he 'sold' the package correctly, his members would finally accept about forty per cent less than they had been demanding and that management would have reached agreement at some seventy per cent of what they were really able and willing to pay.

If he could keep within those parameters, his negotiations would always succeed.

He armed himself with reasoned arguments to put to the bosses, having already privately acquired their balance sheets to assess just how far they might be prepared to go.

It usually worked and he was highly regarded and trusted as a negotiator by both sides... until, that is, until a rather tricky and unplanned incident put him on the spot.

The main fabrication shop at UnitedMotors was Dickensian, in common with much of Britain's industrial heritage of the early 1960s. It was dark, hot, and fume-laden. During a heat wave the day shift demanded ventilation. Having at first refused to even consider the matter, management then offered to commission a feasibility study.

The temperatures rose and the day shift promptly knocked huge holes in the walls of the factory. They were immediately suspended and Jack went to see the industrial relations manager, a former colonel, to notify him of an unofficial strike. The colonel replied that he hadn't spent 'three bloody years in Burma' to be told what was or was not hot weather. If the day shift didn't clock on next morning, he'd fire 'your whole bloody tribe of Commie mates.'

Late into the night, in the smoke-filled, sweaty conference room of the union, Jack and the men's stewards argued – unaware that, even as they spoke, something dramatic was happening back at UnitedMotors.

The night shift had found the assembly shop unacceptably cold and had walked out in unofficial action pending the installation of heaters. The colonel refused and promptly suspended the other half of the company's work-force!

Telephone lines were overloaded. Trades union shop stewards were asking their regional and national officers for guidance while the colonel was frantically contacting the Motor Builders' Federation and the Confederation of British Industry for advice.

Short of having a building team on hand to knock-down and rebuild walls every time there was a temperature change, UnitedMotors couldn't act. Even worse, other industries saw the dispute as the planned flare path leading towards a national strike and were happy to distance themselves and leave it to the colonel to sort matters out.

Jack was similarly cut adrift by his union colleagues. They argued that if the dispute wasn't settled, dockworkers should be called on to black exports of UnitedMotors' vehicles and then to strike in sympathy, as a mark of solidarity, in a disruption that was as unplanned, unwanted and feared by the trades unions as it was by the employers. Even worse, with Jack Huggins involved, any support at national level would imply that the trades unions were now in the hands of the Socialist Workers' Party and the hard left.

His negotiating skills were put to the test. On the trade union maxim of divide and conquer, he put it to the day shift that their overnight comrades were risking the day shift jobs by their unilateral action. There was no way this betrayal of comrade by comrade could be defended.

He put the same argument to the night shift, adding – for the first time – that he thought there might be some room for manoeuvre. He asked them what they would accept... and then went back to the day shift with this information to ask for their views.

Both shifts agreed that he should talk to management and sound out their proposals for a possible resolution of the dispute.

He did, but not before a long session with the Health and Safety officer.

The colonel was in a more accommodating mood than usual. Instead of offering Jack the usual bottle of warm beer from a crate in the outside office, he asked if he'd like a scotch or a glass of chilled wine. Jack shuddered – 'that man just doesn't know his arse from his elbow' he thought, 'fancy trying to bribe me with an executive drink from his office refrigerator. Here we are arguing about temperatures and this prat is more worried about chilled wine, or ice in his scotch.'

'My demands,' Jack said, coming quickly to the point, 'are that my membership shall work in dignity and comfort and that this comfort shall extend equally to day comrades as well as to the night shift.'

The colonel sighed: 'Jack, Jack, we just can't give way on this one. There's no way we can afford new ventilation in the works and, anyway, it would be winter before we could get it installed. And, before you say anything, we're not going to have a team of builders on permanent stand-by to keep knocking a wall down, putting it back up and then knocking it down again every change of shift.'

'I'm not talking about that,' Jack said. 'What I'm suggesting is an agreement whereby the wall stays intact, but there's a fifteen minute ventilation break every time the internal temperature goes above eighty-five degrees.'

'No way,' said the colonel, 'I'm not agreeing to that.'

'You haven't much choice. It's the only deal I can sell to my members. Think about it very carefully.'

Jack went back to the men and outlined his proposals.

'I'm not too sure about winning this one, comrades', he said. 'Management will not accept a fifteen minute break every time the temperature tops eighty-five degrees.'

There were strong murmurs of discontent.

'I'm afraid we may have to agree. Firstly, management are threatening to dock pay from everyone who had a hand in demolishing the wall. If they go to court they could possibly enforce it. But, secondly, from a union point of view, comrades, those who did it are liable to disciplinary procedures including possible suspension if they didn't belong to the Bricklayers' union.'

'Comrade Jack,' said a voice from the smoky haze that screened the back of the room. 'You say that management will not agree to a cooling break at eighty-five degrees. Can we get it at eighty-six'?

'I might get eighty-three and get them to agree to drop the damages claim.'

Delegates authorised the agreement and the colonel accepted it.

Even he hadn't realised that Jack had won an impressive victory in a battle that would never arise.

In his meeting with the Health & Safety officer, Jack had established that the assembly-shop temperature had never been recorded as topping the eighty-two degree mark!

Over the years Jack honed such skills of duplicity until, one day, he was called in by the head of personnel.

'Jack, I want you to be the first to know that we're heading for a thirty percent redundancy and you're in the first group to go. Our contacts have made a few soundings and we don't think anyone'll stand up for you. Your membership says you've been feathering your own nest and we're spreading the word that we won't tolerate a strike. We can't afford it so if we don't get our reduced numbers, hopefully by voluntary redundancy or early retirement, we'll have to close down altogether.

'On the other hand, the colonel is taking early retirement and we're looking for a replacement that knows the industrial relations ropes and is a tough negotiator. We'd let you have your full redundancy package then, after six months, advertise externally. You'd get the job.'

Jack Huggins was not fitted to his new poacher-turned-game-keeper role. In the past he'd been Jack but now he was Mr Huggins. He'd driven his own old Ford; now it was a Rover with a driver. He found a suit and tie more constricting than jeans and an open-necked shirt. Even management training courses were alien to him. No more smoke-filled rooms at union HQ. In their place talk-ins, teach-ins, lectures and seminars at top hotels with the occasional conference in the Bahamas or Florida. Cigarettes, beer and sandwiches had now been replaced by cigars, fine wines, brandy, caviar and canapés.

His old comrades treated him as if he had become a leper. His roughness, bluntness and social awkwardness made him feel out of place with other departmental heads in senior management.

In a way, it was this that took him to Dufftown and his final critical negotiation.

He had married into the family of Captain Angus Lyons. There was nothing wrong there in that Angus had been a chimney sweep when he joined the Royal Grampian Rangers in 1938. He was a real working class hero who, as a severely wounded sergeant-major, had so inspired his outnumbered men at Tripoli that he had been awarded the Military Medal in the field and promoted to captain.

Captain Lyons returned to Dufftown in 1945 to rejoin his three daughters, Margot, Jess and Rose and to become – by unanimous vote – firstly the chairman and later the president of the Royal Grampian Rangers Association, the 'Gramps' as they were affectionately known.

In 1980, in his eightieth year, Angus died.

Jess and Jack and Margot and Tom had homes near each other in Surrey, with Rose and her husband Colin, continuing to live in Dufftown.

Rose and Colin were honorary members of the 'Gramps.'

On the long, sad, journey north for the funeral, Jack had discussed the arrangements with his wife and her sister. Both women loved flowers to such a degree that they were totally against what they saw as 'wasting them in wreaths.' Rose 'though, perhaps because of her name, fancied them in abundance in vases, on tables, in wreaths and on coffins.

At Rose's home in Dufftown, two things were immediately obvious. The first was that the three sisters were a living proof of two being company but three being a crowd. There was never any unanimity of thought and action on anything.

'Have you put Da's funeral notice in '*The Press and Journal*' yet?' Jess asked, 'if not, Margot and I have decided that it should state family flowers only.'

'You can't do that,' said Rose. The 'Gramps' have said that as Da' was their president they're going to send a huge wreath in the regimental colours.'

'But we don't want it. If we let them do it, then other people will want to send flowers and we've already told other friends and relations that we don't want them. If there are flowers from the 'Gramps', then I won't go to Da's funeral,' Margot stormed.

A major row was brewing.

Jack had a sinking feeling that he was going to be drawn into yet another family feud.

Colin turned to him. 'What do you think? Angus was proud of the 'Gramps' and they were proud of him. Rose and I are honorary members so we can't just tell them to stick their flowers. If we did they'd probably chuck us out.'

Margot and Jess stuck to their guns although, in Rose's opinion, Margot was a stupid little bitch if she wanted to argue about flowers instead of seeing Da' to his grave. Margot, on the other hand, was a champion of Da's sense of duty. If they said 'no flowers' then it should be no flowers. What a pity Rose's mouth was bigger than her understanding and acceptance of the feelings of others.

'Jack,' said Colin, 'please sort it out. I've known all of them longer than you. This could easily end up as a brawl in the church.'

Jack decided to telephone the chairman of the 'Gramps,' Hamish Burns.

'Hamish, you don't know me. I'm the captain's son-in-law and I'd like your help. The family have decided that they don't want any flowers other than their own spray of roses and we're therefore suggesting donations to charity instead of floral tributes.'

A slurred voice responded. 'Who did you say you are, laddie?'

'Jack Huggins, the captain's son-in-law.'

'What regiment were you in?'

'None, but I don't see that has anything to do with it. Anyway, I was in the Navy – national service and all that.'

'Oh, I see. And where are you from?'

As soon as he said 'Surrey' he realised his mistake.

'Oh, so you're a gin drinking pooftah sailor from England, then. Now get this straight, laddie, the 'Gramps' are always laid to rest wi' a regimental wreath. It's non-negotiable.'

The line went dead after a heavy 'clunk' followed by the dialling tone suggested the receiver being slammed down.

Jack tried again.

'Mr Burns? Jack Huggins here again about the captain's funeral. Two of his daughters are quite distressed about your decision. Can't you put it to the committee?'

The telephone receiver was replaced again.

Two hours later Hamish Burns telephoned back. If anything his voice was less distinct but more positive and hostile. Jack formed the opinion that the intervening two hours had been spent at the bar rather than with the committee.

'Is that Jackie Buggins? I've looked up the rule book and there's no way out. Rule 17 lays down arrangements for the funerals of ex-

Gramps. Rule 17 (4) says that for each president being laid to rest, there shall be an attendance of at least one officer of the association and five members. The said officer shall wear the regimental tie and a black arm band. The five members – if above the rank of sergeant – shall wear regimental ties. Those below the rank of sergeant shall wear black ties.

'Rule 17 (5) states that a deceased president shall be honoured with a wreath of flowers containing the association's badge, be of a diameter of twenty-four inches and purchased at a cost not exceeding £45, such sum to be met from the special fund of the association.'

This time it was Jack who hung up.

After an hour of thought he attempted to negotiate a way through the impasse.

'Mr Burns? Jack Huggins here. Does the association have a piper?... good... Bearing in mind your rules and the family's wishes, can we meet half way?

'We wondered if, instead of a wreath, the 'Gramps' might see their way to sending a piper to the church to play *'Amazing Grace'* or something similar. It would be a fine and appropriate tribute and, of course, the family would express their public gratitude in the thanks column of *'The Press and Journal'* in due course. As a further gesture they would send £45 to the special fund of the association.'

Perhaps there was an omen in the speed, as well as the manner, with which Hamish said 'Done,' and added 'but our members won't like it one little bit. Rules are rules, laddie.'

Captain Angus Lyons would have been proud and impressed with by his own funeral. There were his three daughters actually on speaking terms; the coffin was draped with the St Andrew's Cross of Scotland; and former comrades – appropriately dressed for the burial of a deceased president of the 'Gramps' – formed a guard of honour.

The family procession entered by the south door of the church but, as they paused to compose themselves, the north door opened and a small group marched in and occupied the space between coffin and family.

At their head a kilted drummer played a muffled roll.

Then came the piper in the full dress uniform of the Royal Grampian Rangers. The music he played was not *'Amazing Grace.'* It was a Highland lament.

But the worst was yet to come in a defiant act of betrayal and the violation of a negotiated solemn and binding agreement.

Between the piper and the coffin came the figure of Hamish Burns almost hidden and staggering under a huge wreath in regimental colours, the badge as its centrepiece.

Jack Huggins still treasures that note of thanks, from Margot, in its green ink.

He has now taken early retirement as an industrial negotiator.

THE PROMISE

[Advertisers sometimes use a mixture of meaningless words or strange statistics to promote their products or services. Those sprays that kill UP TO 99.9% of all KNOWN germs and insects are a case in point. Does this mean that ALL insects escape with 0.1% of their life intact and on a diminished nuisance scale, or that in any group of 1000, one creature will survive? And what is the execution rate for UNKNOWN germs?

Read the label and all its terms and conditions and any promise may well turn out to be either contradictory or rash.

And just how could this one is fulfilled?]

Clearing up after Bernard's death was going to be very harrowing.

His wife of 59 years had, by only a few months, beaten their diamond wedding anniversary and their joint 90th birthday celebrations to the grave. Trying to finalise her affairs would be pretty confusing as, in the six months since her passing, he had tried to reinvent himself as an independent and self-assured individual.

He had started going to computer classes but secretly admitted that it was the company of tutors and fellow young students that was the real attraction. After all, his trusted and reliable Remington portable typewriter had served him well although he was finding it increasingly difficult to get replacement ribbons with black ink at the top and red ink below.

And this was important to him. An accounts manager by training and profession, he was the chairman, secretary, treasurer and executive committee of the residents' association of the small block of flats in which he lived. He was never critical or judgmental of the young and disinterested, but would have given his honorarium with pleasure to anyone willing to take over at least some of the tasks that went with the treasurership. It seemed so unfair that none of the younger residents showed the slightest interest in even attending meetings, let alone becoming an officer.

Not for him the weird metric numbers of today's paper sizes. 'Foolscap sounds like something reliable,' he would say to the totally confused assistant at his favourite stationers. 'A4 is anonymous. It sounds like a trunk road.' He therefore continued to keep the day-to-day accounts in a huge and elderly ledger.

Into that ledger, working from the front, went financial details. Income was entered on one side and expenditure on the other with the carry forward written and underlined at the bottom of the page and then carefully inscribed at the top of succeeding pages. Working from the back of the book, he entered key information of dates for the payment of outgoings such as insurance, maintenance work and submission day for the annual tax return.

In another section he recorded all the quotations that had ever been received from painters, decorators, plumbers, electricians and plasterers for work on the block of flats. Under each contract he not only recorded the agreed price, but the percentage by which unsuccessful estimates had overshot the final figure. Thus, if in 1994, a plasterer who had over quoted by 6% for a job in 1982 put in a tender only 2% more than the lowest for the new work, Bernard might regard this as a sign of competitive contrition and give him the work by way of encouragement!

Once a year the trusted Remington would be carefully taken out of its case. Cushioned from the surface of the kitchen table by four neatly-folded complete copies of the local weekly newspaper, and fitted with a brand new two-colour ribbon, it would be used to produce fourteen individual copies of the annual accounts with debit balances in red, and credits in black.

He would then type personal letters to each member of the association drawing their attention to the forthcoming annual meeting at which the accounts would be presented, and formally requesting their attendance. He would take a carbon copy of each letter, every carbon copy then being be filed for exactly six years.

Bernard might, from all this, sound like a bored old man with little to do and all the time in the world to do it.

He most certainly was not.

He just possessed the ingrained belief of an old soldier that if a strict routine was followed, there was then no chance of something going wrong or of matters getting out of hand.

But, to return to the sorting of effects.

His wife, Phyllis, had died a few months before him. When it was time to clear up her personal possessions, Bernard had examined everything closely before putting it in a plastic bag and labelling it clearly with the date and, as far as he could remember, any explanatory notes.

Many of the items were mementos of past holidays together.

There were photograph albums of Phyllis when they first met. But why, he wondered, were there blank spaces where yellow marks clearly indicated there had once been pictures? Was it that he had replaced a former boy friend in her life? He would never know.

Cream jugs from Llandudno and Yarmouth (slightly chipped), two bright-blue ceramic love-birds (without beaks) from Margate, picture post-cards bought fifty years earlier, faded photographs, an eagle's foot brooch with two claws missing, a charm bracelet with its London bus, Westminster Abbey and folded ten shilling note.

There was a brass mass-produced tourist souvenir of the Eiffel Tower, its somewhat eccentric shape suggesting an imaginative phallic interpretation of the famous inspirational eloquence of the Paris landmark.

There was the woolly hat she'd always worn if it was cold and dry and the little plastic one she used when it was wet. There were her spectacles and – even more poignantly – the camera he'd bought her while they were touring Scotland. It still had a roll of film in it as they'd never worked out how to remove it.

Everything had been meticulously and lovingly recorded and put away.

Now it was time for the executor to go through another collection of belongings and papers a few days after Bernard had died.

There was the regimental tie and the campaign medals from his war-time service, his long-service decoration from the Royal Observer Corps, a pipe (although he had not smoked for forty years), a walking-stick with an Alpine badge on it, road maps and the estimated costs of their motoring holidays and an air timetable for a journey they had never got round to making.

The ruthlessness and feeling of intrusion in going through their personal possessions was overpowering – yet it had to be done and the executor of a Will has no right to become emotional.

Clothes and junk for the tip ... items for the cats' charity shop ... a couple of watches and rings to be valued and recorded.

To Phyllis and Bernard they had been items of memories and love, secret tokens of their feelings – to the jeweller they were trinkets of little cash value.

It was with some relief that the next, and final, task had to be undertaken – the examination of tin boxes of letters and accounts, useless share certificates (of companies long since engulfed by the insatiably grasping onward march of major organisations) passports and driving licences.

From all these records and the carefully logged bank statements and authorisations it was possible to identify, for the purposes of cancellation, outstanding direct debits for rates and insurance, public utilities and their joint long-standing subscriptions to animal and environmental charities.

At last the executor's duty was complete. No stone had been left unturned. It was all neat and tidy. How Bernard would have appreciated it.

Two weeks after the funeral, a solitary letter somehow found its way through the redirection system and was lying on the mat just inside the front door as the executor walked into the former home with an estate agent.

Addressed personally to Bernard, it was from one of those motor breakdown and recovery firms who have advertising tentacles that none may escape.

It said simply: 'Our Promise – We'll find you wherever are.'

They have probably failed.

THE KILLER

[Death can appear in many guises. In some cases the exact cause will never be established and, in the case of some criminal killings, the perpetrator may never even be suspected.]

Satan reigned supreme over two kingdoms.

The point of separation was not a set of pearly gates, but a tubular-steel farm gate with its bars wreathed in barbed wire with a heavy metal mesh hung behind. This barrier of wire and netting encircled '*The Priory*' with an impenetrable barricade which prevented casual entry or access save through the gate. There was, it is true, no real reason why anyone should pass through the gateway without either the invitation or the prior permission of its sole occupier.

A series of marked and locked boxes made it possible for the postman, the newspaper boy, the milkman and the various meter readers to complete their duties without attempting to open the gate with its huge and totally unnecessary warning to 'BEWARE OF THE DOG.' As a further safeguard, an intercom provided a link from gate to house so that even expected callers could make certain that Satan was not lurking somewhere in the shrubbery waiting to put the final snapping touches to a carefully prepared ambush.

Satan was undoubtedly a dog with a personality problem. It hated anyone or any thing in black trousers. Until the town magistrates had ordered it to be muzzled when in public (and the Union of Communications Workers had refused to make any postal deliveries) Satan had waged a one-dog war against all wearers of black trousers, be the offending garments formal or informal, worsted, serge or denim. The waiters at the Chanticleer Chinese restaurant were thus as much at risk as the community policeman or the traffic warden. Postmen, even the St John Ambulance Brigade collectors, firemen and the town band could all bear testimony to the dog's commitment to savagery in its hatred of sartorial blackness.

Satan, an Alsatian, had been of such horrendous potential in the field of aggression and viciousness that his original owners, having been suspended and then expelled from dog obedience classes, were more than relieved when he was accepted for training by the police.

Within four weeks the constabulary was asking how much the owners would accept to take the creature back off their hands.

A deal was done and Satan was classified as 'unfit for police duties' owing to a mercurial disposition, an unstable attitude towards its handler and a canine psychopathic disorder manifesting itself against wearers of black trousers.

The unwanted dog was just what Miss Letitia Smyth-Thompson required.

'The Priory' was a large rambling house left to her by her late father, a wealthy solicitor.

Regarded by many as eccentric, her home reputedly held hundreds of thousands of pounds in cash and valuables. With a high local burglary rate, occasioned by the drug-purchasing habits of many of the town's less reputable youngsters, her insurance company warned her that they could no longer grant her anti-intruder cover without enhanced security.

Alarm bells and burglar alarms would not be enough, she was told. There was always the possibility of someone attacking her while she tended the plants in her wilderness of a garden and then of forcibly using her to reveal where anything of value was hidden.

Vagrants, too, sometimes invaded her garden and either vandalised greenhouses and outbuildings, smoked strange substances in the potting shed or held pagan bonfire rituals in the overgrown jungle which surrounded *'The Priory.'*

It was Constable Barker who suggested that if she really wanted an all-round companion and security guard, he knew just the one for the job – Satan.

It was love at first sight. She had been a Lieutenant-colonel in the Military Police, was chairman of the county magistrates, a deputy lieutenant of the county and a prison visitor. An ex-police dog would be ideal and, with her attitudes to discipline, she would soon conquer its waywardness.

There was an immediate bond of mutual respect and trust. Satan would gladly accept the confinements of his muzzle on the town side of the gates if he was given total freedom to wander at will through everything on the inside. The muzzle, the dog discovered, was only a slight encumbrance. With a combination of sheer power and weight he could escape his leash whenever it suited him and could still bring terror and mayhem wherever he chose.

And as for the garden, well Satan knew the law and liberally interpreted 'reasonable force' as carte blanche to savage intruders at will. He was a potential killer. He knew it, Letitia knew it, Constable

73

Barker knew it, that huge dog was an executioner in waiting. It could only be a matter of time.

John Peters had many things on his mind that afternoon. Newly ordained, he had been appointed curate at the parish church two weeks earlier. His self-appointed duty would be to increase church attendances. His strategy was simple. If he could find one or two non-attendees and persuade them to come, and then get them to return the following week with a friend, the snowball effect would show a rapid and increasing level of success.

He looked at the fortress-like entrance to '*The Priory*' and opened the gate without his preoccupied mind fully registering the warning about the dog. He had, in any case, seen several similar enamelled plaques with comparable warnings. Usually the so-called dangerous dog was nothing more than a geriatric terrier or a fluffy unidentifiable bundle more likely to trip a visitor as, in search of affection, it carried out a ritualistic figure of eight movement around – and between – the legs of strangers.

He had only once encountered a really hostile canine intent on killing or maiming. It was not a happy recollection and he pushed the incident to that tiny private compartment of his mind in which were stored those memories he would rather forget in the fullness of time.

As he walked up the laurel-lined drive he held his Bible prominently in his right hand.

Together with his very obvious clerical garb, the Bible acted as a usually accepted proof that he was not trying to introduce the householder to one or other of what he regarded as the bizarre beliefs dispensed by other doorstep evangelists. It was a Bible that had seen him safely through several near-death experiences in his previous calling.

Smelling the honeysuckle, marvelling at the navigational skills of the bees and the untiring industry of the ants, he was alarmed by an intrusive sound. It was the threatening bark of a large dog crashing its way through the bushes and making towards him. Before he could move, it was on him in a confused jumble of hair, fury and snapping teeth. It slobbered thick saliva and its eyes seemed to burn with the fire of catherine wheels gyrating in full fiery rotation.

Its bites were so rapid that they did not register individually. It ripped his leg, savaged his knee and tore into his hand as he tried to push it away. Then it pulled back on its haunches ready for a jump at his throat.

His reaction was automatic, immediate and successful.

The front door of the house opened as John Peters made for a safe haven.

As Letitia had said so many times before to other victims: 'I'm most dreadfully sorry. Satan has a thing about people in black trousers but he's never behaved like that before.

'Come in: let's see if I can sort you out. Would you like a cup of tea or a coffee, padre, or possibly something a little stronger while I try to find the first aid box?'

'Padre?' he thought. 'Sounds like someone with a military background.'

He opted for a whisky. He needed one while he tried to work out just why he hadn't assessed the probability, direction and ferocity of the dog's attack.

As Letitia used warm water, a large bottle of TCP, cotton wool, lint and bandages to clean and dress his wounds, he asked her about her use of the word 'padre'.

'Do you have an army background?'

'Yes,' she said, 'although you mightn't believe it. I made half colonel in the Military Police. Why did you home in on it?'

'You used the word "padre" when you spoke to me and I put two and two together.'

Letitia was impressed.

'In a way we were in the same job,' the curate said. 'I was in the SAS so I was taught to evaluate words and situations quickly just like you Red Caps. After all, my life could have depended on my split second decision on how something was going to develop and then taking pre-emptive action.'

'Well you weren't very good with Satan, were you?' she challenged good humouredly.

He looked down at his injuries and shredded trousers. 'No. I admit I wasn't concentrating that time and I paid the price.'

'What sort of tasks were you doing?'

John Peters knew that, as a former SAS lieutenant, he could not talk in detail to anyone about any of his missions.

'Oh, a little of this, a little of that. Getting into places like Afghanistan and Iraq and taking out the occasional trouble-maker.'

'Taking out? You mean kidnapping?'

'No, taking them out as in the case of personal elimination. Sometimes it was a gun, other times it was with whatever was handy, like a stone or a hefty piece of wood. One of the most effective tools I used was a rolled newspaper with a fine sheet of toughened steel between the pages to strengthen it.

'It was the killing that I eventually found so repugnant that I came out a couple of years ago and decided on a career in the church. Instinctive and violent action had become a fact of life, either them or you. The living I could accept, but the alternative appalled me.'

They talked for another hour or so. Letitia even agreed to come to church with, as she put it, 'at least two friends to give you a float.'

It was time to go.

'I'll walk down to the gate with you. As soon as Satan sees us together he'll know you're no threat if you should call again.' She called the dog, but there was no reply. 'He's probably hiding somewhere or gone off looking for intruders,' she said, 'I wonder where he is?'

'Probably on his way to hell,' John thought as he felt the reassuring stiffness of the wafer of strengthened steel that ran reassuringly down the spine of his Bible and he paused to wipe the matted blood and hairs from its cover.

THE WORDSMITH

[Although the professions of blacksmith, locksmith, silversmith and goldsmith have an understandable and recognisable status, one smith is missing from the list – the wordsmith. Despite this omission, the wordsmith is in full employment wherever and whenever words are required or used.

The wordsmith shares the craft of the illusionist in creating magic out of the mundane; of the water diviner in producing humour in an arid place; and of the carpet maker in turning dull skeins of wool into a rich tapestry of design.]

There were times when even Robertson Byrne fully accepted that there were no such things as so-called 'natural writers.'

In reality, authors are no more than adept exponents of the craft of wordsmithery. Given that tens of millions of nouns, verbs, adverbs and adjectives are used in the every-day presentation of the spoken or written word, then the uniqueness and success of any writer lies in the sequence in which words from that existing stock are reshuffled and re-presented in a different format. In simple terms, nobody adds to the colours and textures that have been built into a kaleidoscope yet, by twisting the body of the instrument, a virtually non-repetitive series of patterns can be created.

So far, so easy. So easy, so simple. Or so the logic would seem to run. Yet even the accomplished wordsmith has to deal with an extra dimension. Words are of themselves devoid of warmth, feeling and understanding. The writer must therefore find a distinctive style in using familiar words to express sentences and reactions in a way that do not seem obvious, predictable or insincere.

Take the case of Robertson Byrne. In terms of the spoken word, he knew the right verbal buttons to press to gain both the interest of, and an advantage over, any woman who took his fancy at the key moment of any emotional vulnerability she might be experiencing. Age, morality, class or background played no part in this. It was all part of a general game of wits and challenge in which Robby had every intention of being the winner as often as possible.

He was able to read any warning signs and therefore mostly managed to avoid making a fool of him by sensing what *not* to say when the lady in question was expecting a predictable onslaught on her emotions from every man she met at the time.

Age made no difference; he had absolute confidence in his own attractiveness to women. As an older and, in his own opinion, a more mature man, he believed he could put on the cloak of paternal protectiveness or the mantle of a wise and trusted friend. Who would ever suspect, until too late, that he had a hidden agenda of conquering challenge? Age could therefore be used as a key weapon in his armoury.

So too, he believed, could the fact that he was only of moderate height and rather overweight.

Too old? Too fat? No, experienced usage had told him that there was only one real handicap – the excessive mileage of his body machinery. In the course of his life he had ruthlessly used every imaginable combination of words for flattery or seduction, commiseration or congratulation. He now realised that his chat-up lines were as dead as the Dodo and that his techniques owed more to the films of the 1970s than the reality of 2005.

Against this background, Robby (well on the way to his seventy-third birthday, carrying too much fat and light years shorter than any modern maid teetering atop such high heels that an oxygen mask should have been a fashion accessory) met Ludmilla Yuzhanov.

It was not a case of love at first sight (especially on her part!). Having met her he admitted to a feeling of wishing that he could shed at least two stone, extend his legs by about four inches and talk more freely about a wide range of topics as a prelude to serious motivated chat-up.

Ludmilla was about the same height as him, of wonderful proportionate build, probably in her late twenties. She was intelligent and humorous in her conversations which encompassed a wide range of fascinating topics. She had arrived at the college where he was studying computers, from her native Russia via America.

His interest in her was aroused. He was mesmerised by her soft shoulder-length black hair and her challengingly mocking voice (Tchaikovsky could have dedicated a symphony to her just using the subtle character and inflections of her voice while she was speaking.)

The voice had the deep tonal quality of an English-speaking Russian, with each syllable of every word rounded and perfectly presented. She was as beautiful to the ear as she was to the eye.

Even these striking qualities could not match the classic beauty of her eyes. They were dark, mysterious and cavernous and, like music, could portray humour, deep thought or, as he was to find later, the most profound and haunting unhappiness he would ever see on a human face.

There was another point of interest – she was a qualified engineer.

Ludmilla flattered him. She seemed interested in his conversation. She made him feel special and he believed – or at least hoped – that he amused and interested her. It seemed to him that they jousted with words and thoughts rather than just uttering them. Often she got the better of him in their exchanges; yet he was surprised (and not unhappy) to find himself the target of her wit. Humour was something they could share; laughter was the one exclusive personal gift he could offer her.

How he wished that they could spend just one evening together over a meal as friends. She was such an enigmatically interesting person who willingly offered and shared a wide range of knowledge and interests.

Robby's attraction towards Ludmilla grew. He attempted to grasp a few words of Russian to show his seriousness to learn more. His poor memory for words and his pronunciation usually reduced her, privately, to laughter. '*Ty glupy stary durak*,' she would say affectionately without explaining that she was really calling him a stupid idiot. Her laughing eyes told him that, whatever the words meant, there was no hurt or rudeness intended.

Although realising that feelings were very much a one-way traffic between himself and the alluring creature from St. Petersburg, Robby allowed himself the one tiny exciting luxury of believing that a fraction of what he felt was returned.

Persevering with his determination to master a few words that would show he had a more than passing interest in their friendship, he moved on to '*ty mne vy ochen' nravishsya.*' Ludmilla smiled her thanks: '*spasiba*' Thank goodness he had only tried to say 'I like you a lot.' Had Robby said that he loved her ('*ya lyublyutibya*') she would, she knew, have had to end his fantasy and put him firmly in his place with '*eta nevazmozhna*' ('it's not possible.')

The realisation of just how impossible it was that things could flourish between them came one earth shattering and hope-destroying day he would always remember.

They met. They exchanged the non-sensual courtesies of kisses on each other's cheeks. He noticed that her eyes were sparkling brighter than he had ever seen them shine before. She had an air of total confidence and sublime happiness.

'I know you are a writer,' she said. 'I have for you a beginning to a lovely and romantic story.

'There is a soldier; well he is a sergeant in the Royal Marines. On training in Egypt he has hurt his leg and been granted a two-day break from duty to get it strong. With only a few hours off duty, he has still flown to England and telephoned his girl friend's house. He speaks to her friend, Cleo, and tells her that when, later, someone comes to the door she must see that his girl friend opens it so he can give her a surprise and they can spend time together. He has travelled all this way so they can be together for a few hours.

'Surely that is a romantic story of true love on which you can write?'

As he looked at her face he realised that it was more than the plot of a story. Ludmilla had gently found the time and the words to let him know that she was not looking for male company as she already had a boyfriend who would literally travel half way around the world to be with her.

Robby avoided her for three weeks.

Although he could not explain why, he had a strong feeling that he wanted to see her just once more before trying to sweep her out of his life. It was almost, he felt, as if she was desperately crying out into space for some sort of help.

He went out of his way to see her.

'How are things going?' was the only question that came into his head. How unbelievable. Here he was, a wordsmith with millions of words at his command from which to choose, yet he could only think of a mere four. Perhaps he didn't want to know about her romance. Yet, on the other hand he did! Only by knowing the truth could he begin the painful task of pulling down the shutters on an affair that had never existed beyond his own mind. But surely he hadn't imagined that there was some sort of mental link between the Russian girl and him through which he could intercept what he recognised was a remote cry for assistance of some sort.

There was no kiss on the cheek. Something cautioned him that such a familiarity would be inappropriate. Even before she spoke, he knew that all was not well. Her eyes were strangely lifeless and remote like those of one who has passed through a deep personal trauma from which the throbbing is still seeping like a discharge from an open wound.

'I no longer have a boy friend or my other friend,' she said simply. Her eyes told of the anger and painful feelings of betrayal and hurt she was enduring over whatever it was that had taken place.

Whenever Robby was at a loss for words he would try to overcome his inadequacy by asking others to talk. 'What happened?'

'It was the second night he was back. I was studying a little late. When I got home I found three empty wine bottles on the downstairs table. I thought he had gone on up to bed as he had to be up early for his flight back to Egypt.

'I went upstairs quietly. There were two bodies pulsating in my bed. I didn't know what to do so I went down again. When I went up a little later, they were still doing it.

'I shouted "Atebis, zalupa!" They didn't understand Russian, but they got a pretty good idea of what I was saying, climbed out of bed, dressed and left together. Now I have no boy friend and I have lost my other friend as well.'

Robby wanted to reach out to her, to hold her, to hug her gently but reassuringly and protectively. He was aware of his inadequacy as he was afraid that this might be mistaken as an attempt to create a physical manipulation of her vulnerability. He held back, hoping he would find the right words with which to tell her that he could recognise her feelings and only wished he could help. How totally helpless he felt. He could understand and share her anger. Indeed, how could anyone have so abused Ludmilla, so violated her trust and left her with such a brooding anger?

It would, however, not be too wide of the mark to believe that Robby was not also considering whether or not this might be a heaven-sent opportunity to perhaps at least ask her for a date so they could chat, and perhaps laugh together once more, over a meal. Indeed, an evening with her would not be an unattractive proposition. She needed to smile again and it was possible that she had told him of her plight because she thought he might be able to bring a little conversational fun back into her life.

Perhaps sensing his thinking, she dashed Robby's hopes to the ground.

'Anyway, I've got a date tonight for a Japanese meal with a dinosaur. He's quite old, thirty-six, and he says that when he's lost two stone he's going to propose.'

'Will you accept?' Robby asked, realising that on Ludmilla's system of progressive mathematics he must, at seventy-two, be classified as a double dinosaur.

'Do you mean the meal or the proposal?' she asked. 'Yes to the first, and probably no to the other. He is so keen that he drove down from Bristol just to take me out for a coffee. It was a round trip that took him over five hours.'

Robby butted in: 'That tells me three things. Firstly, he finds your company as beautiful as your appearance and nature; secondly, he either has a good mileage allowance or a company car; and thirdly that the coffee in Bristol can't be very good!'

For the first time a fleeting smile crossed her face like the first ray of sun peeping down through a grey sky as rain clouds begin to thin and disperse after a deluge.

'Well, the dinosaur's not the only one who wants to take me out. There are several others so I'll see how things go.'

Robby thought deeply. This was the best chance but also the worst time to raise it; there would possibly never be another such moment: 'I'm sorry that you think of men half my age as dinosaurs, because I'd have liked to ask you out for a McDonald one evening if you'd care to come.'

For a moment that old twinkle lit up those beautiful eyes. '*Eta vazmozhna*' ('it's possible') she said. 'After all, a girl has to eat.'

Robby Burns is now reviewing his seductive conversational strategies in the hope she will eventually accept. He has already learned that 'double' in Russian is '*dvaynoy*'.

He has not yet found 'dinosaur' in his phrasebook.

He would be wasting his time, 'though. Ludmilla has now found solace in the arms of a man some eight years her junior. What is the Russian word for 'dinosaurette?'

THE ABSENTEE

[During those 'twixt-world half conscious moments of emerging from a deep sleep, the mind can lose its orientation and slip out of gear by a cog or two.
The results can be quite surprising.]

The moment the alarm clock started its intrusive and aggressive buzzing, Johnnie Stephens knew it was going to be a terrible day.

From the warmth of his bed he could hear the threatening duet of strong winds and driving rain jostling one another into a rich competitive crescendo before diminishing to a deceptive passage of seeming calm. It was December and, he instinctively knew, those unwelcome meteorological duettists were playing to an audience of chilled leaves in running and overflowing gutters.

He heard his mother call up the stairs. It was the same reveille every morning: 'Johnnie, it's five past seven. Time to get up.'

As usual she had, last thing the previous night, laid out his clothes in a neat pile with washed socks and freshly-laundered and ironed underpants, vest, shirt and handkerchief on top of his pressed trousers.

He looked towards the pile, sat up, poked one foot cautiously from beneath the duvet, sampled the coldness of the room ... and restored it to the warmth of his bed until the inevitable second call from downstairs: 'Johnnie, it's half past seven. You must get up now if you're not going to be late.'

At seven forty-five the smell of cooking bacon and egg and tomato wafted upstairs. His mother hated seeing tomatoes change from their healthy red to a congealed blackened mess. She said nothing, 'though, as it was always important to keep Johnnie happy if there wasn't to be a last minute outburst of anger and resentment at having to go to school.

Ten minutes later breakfast was on the table. There was still no Johnnie to eat it. Indeed, while there was usually the sound of him trampling angrily around the bedroom upstairs on days of protest, there had still not been a positive sound from her son that morning.

She made her way loudly upstairs and hammered upon his bedroom door like some invading general knocking at the portals of an enemy-held castle and demanding no less than total surrender.

'I'm not going to call you again,' she said. 'Get up right away, put your clothes on and come right down otherwise you'll be late for school. I'm not going to make excuses for your absence yet again.'

But Johnnie had come to a positive decision. No matter how much his mother might rant, he was definitely not going back to that hell on earth ever again. He had endured enough of all those dreadful kids, horrible meals, overbearing teachers, tests, rules and regulations. It was time to take a stand.

'Johnnie, you'll be late. If you skip breakfast you can still just get there in time.'

'No, mother, I'm not going to school ever again. Anyway, why should I?'

'Because, Johnnie, you're the head teacher.'

THE PHOTOGRAPH

[It was Doctor Samuel Johnson who, when writing to James Boswell in 1780, said: 'Sir, among the antifactuosities of the human mind, I know not if it may not be one, that there is a superstitious reluctance to sit for a picture.'

Peter Swanning had never heard of either Johnson or Boswell and it's doubtful if he had ever encountered an 'antifactuosity' in his life. Despite this he would certainly be able to relate to the wisdom of a superstitious reluctance to pose for a photo.]

Trethew Manor is one of those pseudo 'historic' buildings that are an obvious denial both of history and tradition.

Reputedly it had been the Elizabethan home of the Trethewey family and built from the proceeds of privateering in the honourable cause of filling the insatiable coffers of the treasury of Queen Elizabeth. According to the brochures (with much use of those key legally cautious words 'in the style of') it boasted all its original historic features including, of course, the inevitable bedroom in which the queen had slept.

In reality, this 'in the style of' was a description that fell little short of the ingeniously miraculous since the building dated only to the early 1800s when it had been built as a large farm house. A century later, to avoid the costs of renovation to sidestep a closure order being put upon it as unfit for habitation, it mysteriously fell down – allegedly due to the curse of the Tretheweys, but more due to the ravages of death watch beetle. According to local knowledge, the collapse had been hastened by carefully sawing through several main structural beams and supports.

In the 1930s a football pool millionaire restored the farm and changed the name from Trethew farm to Trethew Manor. Four decades later it conveniently caught fire just before its owner's impending bankruptcy. The insurance settlement was sufficient to create a 'typical Elizabethan manor with guest facilities.'

American tourists loved it. The quaint juxtaposition of a traditional Elizabethan bedroom with blackened plastic beams, a Habitat plastic four-poster bed with patterned curtains by Liberty, telephones (by Sony) designed as rams' horns and en-suites complete with bidet and jacuzzi must have given the Americans a deep and unforgettable hands-on insight into how the Elizabethans lived.

However much cynics, historians and conservationists might scoff, Trethew Manor became a gold-mine mecca – a sort of living El Dorado – for its owners and the American Corporate taste. Any organisation wanting a training day, a strategy conference, a planning symposium or a prestige reception would literally fight to be able to book one of the 'banqueting suites' at Trethew.

The never-ending sequence of weddings, birthdays, conferences, dinners and receptions were a gold-mine, too, for local photographers. Not only did visitors wish to be associated with the place – they demanded a photograph of their shared moment of history and culture as a memento.

It was at Trethew that Peter Swanning and Joanne were introduced to a moment of chilling challenge that would press the genuineness of their love to its greatest test.

Peter's company, the InterTwine Corporation of Atlanta, Georgia, booked Trethew for a marathon European bonding symposium at which senior executives were encouraged to mix and mingle with their opposite numbers over a round or two of golf, a few lengths of the swimming pools, a walk in the hills, or a spot of shark fishing.

There was always a break for morning prayers and a moment of silent unity with family members left at home. Indeed, InterTwine's corporate logo was of a rather fleshy-looking heart pierced with an arrow marked 'loyalty.' The company motto was 'bonded in loyalty and love.' The words 'loyalty in love, love in loyalty' made a bold statement in the centre of the six links of a symbolic chain around the symbolic heart.

InterTwine prided itself on its family ethos. As the president, Cyrus P Schneider, told the opening session: 'We start with unswerving loyalty to our own personal family; we extend that loyalty to our corporate family; and then we proudly carry it forward along the path of our solemn duty towards our consumer family.

'If anyone betrays one of those three sacred links, then they break our great chain. There is no place for moral traitors within InterTwine. We demand total morality within the family and morality in all our corporate and commercial dealings.'

Peter, the Executive vice president for the UK and Ireland was literally the 'home host' since he lived in a small town just down the road from the venue.

Cyrus readily agreed to Peter's suggestion that it would make sense for Joanne and himself to stay at Trethew for three nights. Although Peter was virtually a non-drinker, a combination of organisational responsibilities, socialising and being – as he put it – 'on parade most of the time' justified his stay.

Joanne was delighted when he told her. She'd heard of the romantic history of the manor, of the tapestry-curtained mahogany four posters and the jacuzzis. She'd been told of the thick walls that rendered lovemaking a loud and uninhibited (but sound-insulated) pleasure.

They arrived and checked in.

While Peter went through his check-list of spotlights, microphones, projectors, charts, name tags and information packs in the conference suite, Joanne prepared their bedroom for three nights of romance.

Their sexual bonding, as well as the seminar, was a memorable success.

The final evening was both anticipated yet tinged with sadness. There had been two days of successful bonding and programming for InterTwine's executives. Cyrus was delighted with Peter's organisation of the event and hinted that he would be in line for 'task elevation' to the post of senior Executive Vice President (administration) in Atlanta within six months.

That was the corporate outcome of the seminar. But, for Peter and Joanne, there was the private pleasure and success of three long nights of energetic and uninhibited passion that had surprised as much as it had delighted and exhausted them both.

On top of that would be their new life together in Atlanta.

One formal function remained – the president's reception.

Peter was dressed in a trendy dinner suit that revealed a youthfulness and trimness that she had never noticed before. She found his presence at her side to be arousing and exclusive. Her expression uttered the stark warning to the other wives 'hands off, he's all man – and he's all mine.'

She wore a simple black dress, its plunging neckline brought to a tantalising end by a tiny scarlet rose. She had always known she was attractive to men. The way the heads of the wives as well as the husbands turned showed she had only been half right!

There was a line of guests ahead of them stretching to the president's welcoming hand.

Cyrus P Schneider knew all his executives and their partners by name, it seemed. It was a clever ploy. As he greeted them personally, the local photographer had plenty of time to line up his shot for the obligatory memento of the stay at Trethew.

The repeated flashes of the photographer's equipment had a mesmerising effect on Peter, Joanne noticed. Upstairs in their bedroom, between bathing and dressing, he had shown a loving tenderness in their passionate intimacy. Yet now it seemed as if aloofness had set in. She couldn't define it, but it was as if he was drawing a protective veil around himself... a veil that excluded her.

Joanne took Peter's hand reassuringly and snuggled lovingly into his side. Then, as if this might appear too restrained and contrived a pose for the photograph, she slipped an arm around his waist.

To her disappointment and surprise, Peter edged slightly away as if to make himself remote and unwelcoming of so obvious a display of loving affection. He grew even more agitated: 'I hate these photos, they're no more than moral blackmail,' he said.

'In what way?'

'Well, it's like this,' he said, becoming more disturbed than she had ever seen him. 'All the photos go on show in the photographer's window in Fore-street until they're either bought or eventually replaced by pictures from the next function.'

'You mean,' said an alarmed Joanne, 'your wife might see one?'

THE LETTER

[Let's face it; the ageing process gradually eats into us all. We forget things; we become confused. Even worse, it may not be too long before we send befuddled letters to our lifelong friends like this one from Charlie to Gordon.]

Dear Gordon,

Thank you for your letter. I seem to remember that it amused me very much and that I found it very funny indeed.

Oh dear! I hope it did come from you and not from somebody else. I think I recall looking at it and recognising your hand-writing.

On second thoughts, I'm not sure it was a letter at all. It may have been an e-mail. If that was the case, there was no envelope with writing to recognise so it possibly didn't come from you at all and perhaps I've either not thanked whoever it was, or written to you already.

I think it was Alan Bennett who wrote about the seven ages of man. If it was Bennett, and not Georgina Cookson, they forgot age 6(a) – the forgetful and confused one. I sometimes think I'm in it, but then, again, perhaps not.

Someone told me, or possibly I read it, that many of those born before 1936 are falling victim to an undiagnosed bug known, medically, as the 'Senile Virus.' I can't be certain but as this is 2006 and I am said to be 73, then I could be a sufferer. There is no cure as the elderly scientist who discovered the strain turned 73 before he finished his research into this disturbing and distressing complaint and apparently forgot what he was investigating.

Dreadfully sad when you come to think about it. Quite a loss.

Sometimes I send off blank letters; sometimes I send letters back to the people who sent them to me; sometimes I post them before I've finished and signed them.

Even those young ladies with clipboards who once wanted to know my views on current events or to lure me to hotels to talk about buying a villa in Spain rush away when I tell them that Clement Atlee was wrong to invade the Panama Canal; that Harold Wilson pretended to have drowned himself when he was on holiday in Austria; or that I once had a photograph of General Franco. Try as I may, I can't remember where that photo went or even why I had it in the first place.

I heard one of these young women say to her colleague: 'God grant him the senility to forget those he never liked anyway; the good fortune to run into those he does like; and the eyesight to be unable tell the difference.' I didn't really understand what she meant, but I'm sure it was well intended.

It's a funny thing, memory.

I don't ever remember being absent minded – except, that is about small things.

I know where my glasses are but I can't get to them as they're in the car. I can't get into the car because I've lost the keys. And even if I found the keys, it wouldn't help very much as I just can't remember exactly where I left the car!

That polite young man at the station booking office was helpful when I asked for a senior citizen's ticket. As I couldn't remember where I was supposed to be going, he sold me a return ticket so I'd get back here without too much trouble. I think he was a young man, but he could have been a woman – one gets so confused nowadays.

I don't remember getting forgetful – except, that is, about small things. Or have I told you that already, Ernie?

I had a turn last week or, now I try to remember, it was possibly last month.

Several times I've taken Buster out for his morning walk while still wearing my slippers!

Now, it seems, I've gone one better. We set off and walked for a couple of miles yesterday, me talking to him all the way. Great pal he is, very wise and never argues. I have to keep him on a lead at all times, 'though, as he sometimes gets forgetful and wanders off.

It was only when I got home and hung up his lead that I found I hadn't taken him out in the first place at all. I wondered why he wasn't pulling and wanting to stop at every corner.

I had a chat with a vicar last week. No, I think he may have been a rabbi. No, I definitely remember, she was a major in the Salvation Army. She told me that I had to realise that I was in an age rut and that a rut could eventually become a grave – depending on my perseverance.

She was wise, if I haven't told you this before, Keith, and said I should consider the hereafter. She's right, I go somewhere with the intention of buying something and when I get to the counter I wonder what I'm here after.

Anyway, John, I hope this letter gets to you safely. I am sorry if I should forget to put a stamp on it. I will try to remember. Strange, try as I may I don't recall when I started becoming being absent minded.

Mind you, losing my memory isn't a bad thing as long as there are kind people around who want to help. So many of my old friends are dieing, they tell me, that I ought to get a new black tie. I saw one in Help the Aged for £2 and a couple in Oxfam marked £1 each or two for £1.50. I asked the reason and the very bright young lady in Oxfam said: 'People in the Sudan and Africa don't wear black ties so they're cheap here. But they're obligatory for Help the Aged supporters so they charge more for them than we do.'

I thought she was possibly being a bit cheeky, but I spent £1 on one. I spotted it had a soup stain on it and when I told her, she asked me: 'What do you expect for £1, a caviar stain?'

Perhaps I am getting old and a bit crusty, but I got the feeling she was impatient and being very rude to me.

I really am sorry to ramble on like this. The problem is that I'm never really aware of being a little forgetful until that complete stranger, who says she's my wife, sits me down and sorts things out.

Last week, this woman tells me, I didn't put my letter to you in the right box. As I walked through the park I spotted a little waist-high red box with a black top. I popped it in there. It seems that the picture of a dog and the little plastic shovel chained to the side meant that it wasn't a pillar box after all. Anyway, somebody may have received a real stinker from me. I hope it wasn't you, Jim.

Ever your good friend,
Charlie.

THE AMBITION

[There's a character in the hit American musical 'Chicago' who believes he ought to be called 'Mister Cellophane.' He is of so little value and interest to those around him that he feels that people look through him, rather than at him, and they can't even bother to remember his name.

Had his life not been cut so tragically short by a freak accident, Winthrop K Jones would have regarded Mr Cellophane as an outstandingly successful role model in the world of those who will never throw off the stigma of being leaders in the Society of Anonymous People.]

When passers-by looked into his pram and said 'boo,' he discovered later, it was because he was so tiny and puny as a baby that they feared he might already have slipped into another world. Jokes about throwing the baby out with the bath water became as monotonous to his mother as the repeated suggestions, and advice to her, to put a finer mesh over the outlet pipe of the plug hole 'to avoid a nasty accident.'

At school he was told to wear lead-lined shoes against the possibility of a strong wind toppling him over and never to wear normal loose-fitting shirts for fear of a ballooning lift-off in adverse conditions.

At the cinema his relaxation and pleasure was almost always interrupted when latecomers sliding along the rows in the darkness, with their faces glued to the action on the screen, plonked themselves into his lap thinking it was an empty seat.

He enjoyed the older movies, especially those about the physically or mentally underdeveloped. His favourite was the James Cagney drama, '*White Heat*,' in which the demented and psychopathic Arthur Cody Jarrett, a tearaway social misfit with every problem Freud ever diagnosed, promises his elderly, loving and trusting mother that he really will get to the top one day and finally be recognised.

Six shoot-outs later and the corpses of at least ten cops littering the streets see the renegade standing on top of a huge oil tank as armed police close in. In his one moment of proud achievement, Cagney utters the immortal line: 'Made it, Ma! Top of the world!' Seconds later comes the inevitable explosion which at least launches Jarrett on a spectacularly accelerated upward progress of unrecorded velocity from a static position.

Winthrop found the film melodramatic yet sinisterly funny.

An old American comic dating back to the 1940s, and spotted in a junk shop, gave him fleeting renewed hope one day.

On its back page was the picture of a perfectly muscled man holding the world balanced on his shoulders beneath the words 'Dynamic Tension.' Although not exactly sure just what dynamic tension was, or how to attain it, Winthrop read on.

A smaller picture showed a youth with a retarded physique similar to that possessed by himself. Beside it there was another illustration, this time of seemingly the same youth with three beautiful girls looking adoringly at him. The first picture depicted skinny legs falling out of a pair of bathing trunks that fitted the living scarecrow like a school scarf. The caption ran: 'I was a 98 pound weakling until Charles Atlas rescued me. On the beach they used to kick sand in my face. Just see what Charles Atlas has done for me.'

The transformation was truly miraculous, the bathing trunks now fitted to perfection and added a certain something to the tanned torso by implying that Charles Atlas had eliminated puniness and introduced sexual pulling power.

All this, it seemed, was his for the asking, only a few coins and a plain brown sealed envelope away.

Scanning the pages of the old copies of '*Magnificent Masculine Muscles* & *Beautiful Bulging Biceps,*' he stored under his bed, Winthrop found that the series of advertisements had long since ceased. He suffered despair bordering on a sense of betrayal. Why had fate offered him a destination of hope and then callously destroyed the route map?

He made a definite decision. If bodies depended on fat, sugar, calories, proteins and the like, he'd make that journey. He would eat all the things his mother had told him to avoid. After all, following her example of sensible eating hadn't built him up or caused him to be noticed.

He lived on an unending diet of cheese burgers, crisps, hot dogs and pizzas washed down with lager, sodas and whatever sugar-filled drinks he could get. He munched all the chocolate he could afford. Nothing happened to change him physically although there was the unexpected bonus of increasing the activity of his bowels and bladder.

It was his belief that the 'eat right, stay slim' campaign was an anti-teenager dietary manipulation cause spawned by old people with the intention of making themselves feel virtuous. It was a plot to keep young people like him in a permanent state of skeletal denial and totally unable to make their mark on the world.

Then he hit upon his great idea. It would take a simple design, a special order and the kind of marketing that would make all slim people using his invention appear normal, Winthrop decided. It would be neither more nor less than an inflatable corset that could be worn undetected under normal clothing. It would make him as famous as Charles Atlas.

Eight weeks later he received a large parcel. Only the picture of the little man made out of car and lorry tyres, the name 'Michelin' and the unmistakable smell of vulcanised rubber hinted at its contents. An accompanying letter from Michelin's solicitors informed him that as the pneumatic garment had been personally made to his design and specifications, it was untested. Accordingly neither Michelin or its agents or suppliers could give any guarantee, or accept any liability in the event of failure, accident, damage or misuse.

Struggling into the tight corset-like garment, Winthrop discovered that his bicycle pump was wholly inadequate as a means of inflation.

Waiting until late at night when there would be less chance of being spotted, he went to the filling station at the town's supermarket. He fed a few coins into the air pump, coupled up and waited while a reassuring all-round pressure on his arms and body told him that all was going according to plan.

The first sign that something was amiss came when he was gently raised a few inches into the air and he found that he could no longer reach the off switch on the pump. Compressed air continued to force its way into the bulging creation until – with a loud bang and hiss – the inflator nozzle reached the end of the hose and detached itself from the self-sealing valve.

Gently he rose above the roof-tops, spires and mobile telephone masts into the upper atmosphere where air traffic controllers spotted an object on their radar and issued the only ever navigational warning to aircraft approaching Heathrow of an unidentified human flying hazard. Leaving United Kingdom air space, he made a leisurely journey towards Tibet before his corset was pierced by a small particle of space debris.

Like a demented mosquito experiencing severe flatulence, he circumnavigated the world twice before falling to his death in the Indian Ocean.

Unlike James Cagney, his passing didn't cause a splash (other than in the Indian Ocean). As nobody had ever noticed him when he was alive, a dreadful irony had it that nobody knew he had died! Indeed, had the incident been reported, Winthrop K Jones would probably have been referred to as 'an unknown balloonist.'

And even had anyone noticed his moment of fame, his achievement in making it to the top of the world would have gone unrecorded due to an international one-day strike of all journalists working in the news media.

THE BUTTON

[In the 1960s there was a lawyer-cum-crime writer called Edgar Lustgarten. He also presented a programme on black-and-white television about some of the exhibits in Scotland Yard's Black Museum. These objects had one thing in common: however inconspicuous or meaningless they appeared to the viewer, they had been the key item of evidence that forged the final chain of the link between the crime and the criminal.]

I had picked West Twittering from my carefully researched final shortlist of possible targets.

It seemed ideal for what I had in mind.

The sub-post office was on the outskirts of the town and just three miles away from that magic invisible 'cross-at-your peril' boundary between two rival police forces. It was at the kerb-side where it was possible both to park and to observe the normal comings and goings of its regular trade. As it was only a few yards from the corner, I could be sure of making a quick getaway in the unlikely event of anyone noting my false number plates.

It would be a quick and easy job, really. Pick a day when the Royal Mail van made its weekly delivery of cash and foreign currency, wait until there was the lunch time lull in trade. Put on gloves, pull gun from a Co-Op carrier, point it at the elderly short-sighted postmistress, grab the cash, back to the car and drive off with the loot.

It would be over in seconds and with her poor eyesight there'd be no chance of her positively identifying me.

It all went according to plan – except, that is, for the button. It was a black plastic one made in Walsall. It was about the size of a 1p coin. It had four holes in it. Each of those holes, as I reflected ironically and philosophically later, was equivalent to two years inside one of Her Majesty's less attractive prisons.

It was a pity I didn't spot it as the adrenaline flowed and I gathered up all the cash from the safe and the counter and, for good measure, snatched the tea money. I popped a couple of quid into the animal welfare box on the way out. Nice touch that; my Brief could tell the jury that although I might seem a little unfeeling in robbing little old ladies in post offices, I was certainly not uncaring when it came to our animal friends.

I rammed all the notes into the Harrods bag I'd brought for the purpose. I'm bright, you see. I knew that it would take the Plod quite some time to figure out what kind of armed robber would get his gun from the Co-Op and his groceries in Knightsbridge. That would give me plenty of time to stash the cash well away from home before the Bill turned up on my doorstep.

They'd be bound to take me in for questioning, of course – that was the inevitable downside of having a record like mine for armed robberies on sub-post offices.

Anyway the chances were that they couldn't make anything stick. An almost blind witness, no link with the car, the loot in used notes and, in any case, stashed away in a safe place where I wouldn't touch any of it for several months.

There was so little evidence, in fact, that at first I thought I'd admit to the robbery, then change my plea and wait for the case to be chucked out of Court on the basis of failure to produce enough credible proof of my guilt to convince a jury.

I didn't notice the button amongst the odd loose coins I'd bunged into my pocket.

Did I say 'bunged?' Perhaps 'bungled' would be a better word. That damned bit of plastic was small but it turned out to be significant and incriminating. I must have scraped it up and shoved it into my pocket with all the loose cash.

I wasn't aware of it until the Bill turned my pockets out.

As the forensic guys managed to prove to the satisfaction of the jury, the button the Plod found had come off the old lady's cardigan and must have accidentally dropped into the last handful of coins I grabbed from the counter.

It was a perfect match with the four others still sewn tightly to the garment.

Oh shit, how can I ever hold my head up again?

THE PIG

[Any addict of the square box will know all about so-called 'reality television.'

On the other hand anyone who hasn't encountered this travesty of entertainment must have lived a charmed, sheltered or lucky life.]

I'm getting rather bored by all these so-called 'reality' shows on television.

You know, the sort of thing where electronic technology can recreate the battle of Waterloo before your very eyes, or make the Red Sea roll back so you can cross safely without getting your flip-flops wet.

You can, if you pass the selection auditions, then go on to have an intimate tête-à-tête with Cleopatra (with or without an asp or crocodile as an optional extra); be at the side of King Harold to help a saw-bones pull an arrow out of his eye; or discuss advances in laser haemorrhoid surgery with Napoleon.

The point I'm trying to make, 'though, is this:

When people start using technology as an accessory to entertainment in this way, then it must follow that reality increasingly goes out of the window.

Take one of the new reality television shows – '*An evening with...*'

Just think of the person you'd most like to meet (or least like to meet, as the case may be) in fact, in fiction or out of history. Hand your wish over to the electronic spooks and – Bingo – you can soon be discussing 'this'll kill you' gourmet cooking with the Borgias; 'is height a disadvantage?' with Toulouse Lautrec; or building a simple garden retaining wall with Hadrian.

Name your fantasy and the endless boundaries of technology will soon make it seem a fact.

Frankly, I just don't like the way things are going.

At the press of a zapper button, Judas can be seen delivering pizzas for the Last Supper or the Siamese kings discussing with the pharaohs the comparative merits of honey or black treacle as an active agent in corpse preservation. At a stroke, Salome puts her veils back on, one by one, while, at the same time John the Baptist's head is remarkably restored to his shoulders.

Through special effects and complex graphics, you can create a plausible alternative while you demolish great moments of history.

It just isn't right. Not only is truth distorted, but fiction can be transformed into visual fact while fantasy is given the currency of phoney reality.

I even get nightmares about it, although my psychiatrist has told me there's nothing abnormal in a spot of fantasy (as long as it doesn't involve defrocking nuns or carnal frolics with young nubile uniformed policewomen).

It's not that I'm fastidiously neat and tidy; that I don't occasionally gently turn a plate of cakes so that the one I really fancy is directly opposite myself; or that I don't sometimes use my fingers to cram an awkward bit of food into my mouth when my teeth won't provide a clean cut separation.

No, I don't claim to be a paragon of table-manners virtue.

And that's why the person I'm due to meet in '*An evening with . . .*' fills me with a sickening loathing in his starring and revolting performance as a master of gluttony, greed and social and gastronomic unacceptability.

At first sight he's quite affable. Lives in a house fit for a king, beats me 2–1 in a light-hearted couple of games of tennis, is clearly very proud and protective about his beautiful garden and entertains me at the keyboard with a couple of his latest compositions.

He even lets me look at the family wedding album.

All in all, a pretty genial guy.

But in my nightmare, when all these niceties are over, the television programme producers always make me sit opposite him for dinner.

As I was taught by the social graces tutor at St. Ethelred's, I gently dissect slices of my roast chicken into delicate cubes that can be popped into my mouth and then discreetly chewed and swallowed without so much as a bulge showing in my throat.

He, for his part, rams as much as half the deceased fat-encrusted creature into his mouth. Then he locks his teeth around the carcase and tugs. Some of it comes away and he then wipes his hands (like great shovels they are) on the table cloth as he lays the savaged remnant down when he has gnawed and grunted his way through what is already in, or poking out of, his mouth.

As I delicately sip my wine from a crystal glass, softly savouring each drop, he slurps and slobbers his way through gulps swigged direct from a pewter jug, the overflow dripping down his chin and onto his shirt where it lies in splashes and widening circles.

The nightmare is always the same. It is the same person, the same vulgarity, the same shamelessness and the same revolting performance from him.

And it always has the same ending.

As he belches with the deep rumbling ferocity of a Chinese dragon disgorging subterranean eruptions of foul breath and showering me with morsels of undigested food, I decide that enough is truly enough.

The dream ends as I stand across from him, and sing 'You're the 'Enery I 'ate, you are. The 'Enery I 'ate you are, you are.'

And do you know what happens then?

The bloody viewers always chuck me off the programme and bloody King Henry goes through to the next round!

THE CROWNER

[King Henry VIII was about four hundred years ahead of his time when it came to wheeling and dealing.

Having confiscated Britain's monasteries and abbeys in a bout of privatisation that would be the envy of many a modern government, he then sold the properties and lands to developers in the private sector for either hard cash or favours.

Tavistock Abbey was one such centre of religion… and with it went something that was not Henry's to sell – its history, traditions, folk lore and ghosts.]

He wasn't sure if he'd been awakened by the birds, the bells, the distant babbling and chattering of the fast-flowing river as it leap-frogged huge boulders across the meadow, the chanting, or the daylight sneaking through the latticed window of his small room. It could have been either – or all – of these or even the repetitive habit (he smiled as he always did at that pun) of the disciplines of a lifetime that regularly roused him a moment or two earlier than necessary each morning.

He sniffed the air. His nostrils brought the usual mixed aromas of lavender, apples, rosemary, mint and sage mingling with the sickly smell of the remains of the plump trout on which he had dined the night before.

Today seemed different. Yes, that was it – his first day of retirement as Chief Inspector, Crowner (or Coroner), Tax collector and Constable of the Peace for a division of Devon bounded by the great abbeys of Buckland, Buckfast and Tavistock.

He washed carefully in cold water and, as he mechanically put on his robe and leather sandals, he realised that breakfast would have to be the unattractive but health-giving dish of oats and honey which was the only alternative to what was left of the crusty bread and cheese that had provided a snack during the night.

Clearing room for the empty bowl was a masterpiece of science and planning. Basic laws of housekeeping and area utilisation had long since proved that as space is not infinite, dishes can only be removed from one place if another spot of equal size exists to receive them elsewhere.

His room, he knew only too well, was so small that it could be better described as a cell. At this he allowed himself his second smile of the morning. He, the Chief Inspector, who had dedicated his working life to depriving others of their freedom, lived in a cell himself!

By piling the dishes one upon another, and scraping remnants of fish and other food scraps into a leather bin, he reduced the surface area thus occupied by at least thirty per cent. He found a part-jug of red wine and drank it so he could lay the empty container across the top of the pile. A second jug, this time of rancid repulsive home-made beer, was so disgusting a proposition that he earmarked it for use as a liquid fertiliser and slug-trap on his strip of garden as soon as possible.

This, he felt, was a magnanimously more neighbourly gesture than merely tipping it out of the window when nobody was watching.

He would spend his first day of leisure doing three long-overdue tasks. The floor covering was tattered, worn and discoloured. He would replace it with something more appropriate. Next, he would get to grips with cleaning the chimney, as high as his arm and brush would reach, of the accumulated soot and grime of several unswept years of peat-burning. This, he reasoned, would give greater heat efficiency as well as creating a less polluted atmosphere when, inevitably, winter gales blew smoke back into the room. Finally he would sort out the untidy piles of books and tracts he had acquired with the ultimate aim of entering more fully into the life of the community.

He had barely begun to lift the matting than a visitor approached.

The young man passed under the arch, opened a solid metal-studded gate and scanned several doorways before making his way down the paved pathway between the trimmed lawns, each separated from its neighbour by carefully-pruned knee-high bushes. He walked through the garden and skirted the fish pond before reaching the oak front door. He raised the heavy iron ring that served both as knocker and handle.

He hammered on the door with the solemnity of a judge using his gavel before pronouncing sentence. As the door swung open, the young man stated rather than asked, 'Thomas?'

Assuming that the silence indicated confirmation, he said: 'I'm Paul Arrowsmith from *"The Abbey Chronicle"* and I've been asked to do a story about your life and work.'

115

'You're most welcome, I'm sure,' said Thomas, wondering whether or not he should reveal anything to the young man without prior clearance.

'There I go again,' he thought, 'all those dreadful puns. I talk about habits yet I wear one; I joke about cells when I live in one; and here I am thinking about getting prior approval from the Prior.'

Paul failed to spot the wry smile on his interviewee's face.

'When did you first come to Tavistock, Brother Thomas?' he asked.

'About thirty years ago.'

'Why?'

Because I'd always wanted to become a Benedictine or Cistercian brother and, if you look at the trio of Tavistock, Buckland and Buckfast, you'll see that it's the kind of working environment that's attractive to someone seeking a monastic career – plenty of open space, few distractions and – best of all – a time and distance ruggedness factor that keeps interfering cardinals, bishops and the like well out of the way for at least eight months of the year.'

'But you didn't become a full member of either Order. You went, instead, into the law and order side of things. Why?'

'Frankly, because I realised that I wasn't really cut out to be a sandals and psalms guy – all those early mornings and long days from dawn to dusk with seven prayer sessions a day. And as for Confession, well there was so little carnal mischief that I could get up to, that I had to make up a few to keep the Brother Confessor satisfied that I really was doing my bit and sinning enough to need redemption and forgiveness. Anyway, on top of that, I developed an allergy to concentrated incense.'

Paul was shocked by what he was hearing. He had, it was true, been warned that Brother Thomas was an outspoken character; but this was beyond belief. He had a sinking feeling that the Abbot would slap a prohibition order on the story even before he'd had a chance to write it.

With little optimism that the interview would appear, he persevered – more out of curiosity than for any other reason.

'But why did you cross from Holy Orders to Law and Order?'

'The excitement, the interest and the chance to improve my income,' was the blunt reply.

'How do you mean? I hadn't thought of brothers being interested in personal advancement and financial gain.'

Brother Thomas explained that, in lands owned by the Crown, it was a criminal offence for someone to die by their own hand. Since the law also decreed that nobody should benefit from the fruits of crime, it therefore followed that the funds of anyone committing suicide should go to the Crown and not to the family. To oversee that the worldly goods went in the right direction, the Crown appointed Crowners (later to be known as 'coroners') with the task of investigating any sudden or unexplained death to make sure that assets could be legally sequestered.

Since the abbeys did not possess parallel powers over their lands and tenants, they appointed their own Crowners to seize as much as possible for the abbey funds and to ensure that – under no circumstances whatsoever – anything reached the Crown.

'So I became one of England's first abbey Crowners,' Brother Thomas recalled with pride. 'People soon found that, in exchange for a small contribution towards my retirement fund, a few flasks of wine, a haunch of venison or wild boar, a brace of rabbits or pheasants, there was no such a thing as a suicide on my patch. If someone was found hanging from a tree, my verdict might be that he had overbalanced while trying to fix a washing line for his wife. Slashed wrists were often caused by a moment's lack of concentration while sharpening a bill-hook or a scythe. Stones in the pocket of a body found in the river had obviously been washed in by a swift current.

'In return for a small recognition I was able to record every death as being from natural causes or tragic accident. They were very humane verdicts since, of course, the family kept whatever was left.'

He paused, as if sensing possible danger in the reporter's next question – or of being unwilling or unprepared to answer it.

He was right!

'Given that you admit a willingness to bend the rules, what would you now say was your biggest transgression as the Crowner?'

'It was in the great blizzard of '63. Acting on information received from a certain reliable source, I proceeded to a certain location on Dartmoor where I there found the frozen body of a deceased male person who I now know to have been a hunter from Plymstock, a man named Childe. The deceased person had clearly killed his horse to provide shelter and, using what appeared to have been his own blood, had written a Will. The key sentence of this was that Childe would give all his land and wealth in Plymstock to "the fyrste that fyndes and brings me to my grave".'

Brother Thomas looked thoughtful.

'Here, indeed, was a problem. I had good reason to believe that a search party was already on its way from Plymstock to collect the corpse, bury it there and claim the inheritance. The body lay just outside the jurisdiction of Tavistock Abbey but only a fool would worry about morality when a fortune was at stake. Realising that the Plymstock party would claim the body in order that their community might benefit in accordance with the deceased's wishes, I caused some of the bones of Childe's horse to be placed under a blanket on a stretcher to resemble a body.

'At Yelverton, as I had anticipated, we were intercepted by the Plymstock men. We passed the stretcher to them and bade them well as they took the presumed corpse to their own community to claim their legacy under the unambiguous terms of the Will.

'However, about a quarter of a mile away, a group of helpers from Tavistock were waiting with the real body. We carried Childe to Tavistock Abbey where we buried him and claimed his estate as being the "fyrste that fyndes and brings me to my grave." Once the fuss had died down and everything was tied up, we dug him up and took him back onto the Moor for quite a decent burial under a pile of stones.

'I remember I got quite a good bonus for that little job. Mind you, I haven't dared show my face in Plymstock to this day.'

Uneasy at the way his story was going, Paul Arrowsmith put his next question with caution.

'In the light of what you've just told me, Brother Thomas, did you ever question whether or not you were the right man for the job? You seem to have had a great deal of power... more power, perhaps, than honesty.'

'Of course I was the right man! Who else would have had the guts to take on that dreadful Fitz family? Father and daughter, they were. If ever there was an even nastier chip off a nasty old block, then Josie was it. Came from a rough old line of felons, they did.

'Take her dad, John; his mother and father were warned by the astrologer that he'd turn out to be wicked... and that was six months before he was born! So what did they do? They went to every quack, sorcerer, witch and fortune-teller they could find to change Mother's confinement date to something better. Pills, potions, ointments, oils, incantations, hot baths – none were any good and that evil man was born spot-on under the bad star the soothsayers had predicted.

'He was never argumentative, 'though. Never allowed a quarrel to get out of hand. If he ever even sensed a problem he'd stab the adversary in the back first.'

'How did he get rid of the corpses?' Paul asked.

'Johnnie Fitz'd lay them out along the roadside so we'd think they'd been killed by footpads or highwaymen. I tried to get him the whole time I was Constable of the Peace, but he was always one jump ahead in either killing or scaring my witnesses.'

Paul was intrigued. Brother Thomas had spoken of there being a father and a daughter. 'Tell me about the daughter,' he said.

'Lady Josie, as she eventually became, was a real charmer. She could pull any man she fancied just by using her ''come to bed'' eyes. Then, saying how much her father liked weddings, she'd pretend she was with child and demand marriage. A few months later, with no baby but with a Will in her favour signed and sealed, she'd kill the husband off.

'Like her old man, she was a monster who overcame problems by eliminating them before they became out of control.

'Acting on information received from members of the public, I interviewed her on many occasions about her latest bereavement. She had the cheek to suggest that it was supernatural intervention since they all seemed to disappear into thin air while walking across the Moor at night.

'When I asked why they were walking rather than using one of the several carriages in the yard, she seemed lost for a reply.

'I realised that getting her into the dock for murder would be a waste of time. There were never any witnesses. No matter how much I bribed them, she always offered more. That's the problem of expecting honest policing on the cheap! I changed my tack away from murder and turned to different ground. I said: ''Just now you suggested the coincidental possibility of all your spouses having disappeared into thin air. Does this mean that you believe in witchcraft and the black forces of evil?''

'Too late she spotted my trap. It would be impossible to change her story. I cautioned her: ''Lady Josephine Howard, I am arresting you on suspicion of being an accessory to witchcraft, contrary to Section 13(i) of the Spellbinder's and Evil Doer's Act 1325. You do not have to say anything, but I have to warn you that in the absence of any admission you will be put to the test of ducking. Should you survive three four-minute immersions in a pond while pinioned to a chair, the court may find you guilty of witchcraft and sentence you to death by burning. If, however, your powers of sorcery are insufficient to save you from drowning, then you will be pronounced dead but innocent.''

'To be sure that Josie wouldn't get the easy way out and just drown, I paid the deputy Witch-Prover a few coins to keep immersion times short so I could get her before the Court on sorcery charges.'

With the relish of a man putting the final touch to a pleasurable job well done, Brother Thomas told Paul that Lady Howard was convicted and subsequently put to death by fire on Gibbett Hill, overlooking Mary Tavy. As an eternal penance she was condemned to carry one blade of grass at a time from Okehampton castle to Tavistock until the lawns were bare.

Every night until the end of time, according to Brother Thomas, she has to make that journey in a black coach made of the skulls and bones of her dead husbands and lovers, drawn by headless horses controlled by a headless horseman and with a huge, snarling, black hound in attendance.

'I've recently received information that she drives recklessly, dangerously and at excessive speed across Black Down,' the retired officer told the reporter. 'I must ask my colleagues in Traffic Division to look into it.'

'One final question, Brother Thomas: You've admitted graft, corruption, perjury, perverting the course of justice and conspiracy while holding public office. Does the prospect of death fill you with any apprehension?' Paul asked.

'By Our Lady, no! When I came into this job I was warned that the sure consequence for transgressions on earth would be punishment in the next world through constant exposure to the temptations of sin, adultery, lasciviousness, debauchery, gluttony, drunkenness and the abuse of the body throughout eternity. Just think of it, lad, I can't wait to get there!'

THE SINNER

[Rarotonga is arguably one of the most beautiful islands in the South Pacific. The gentle nature of its people matches the peaceful magnificence of their surroundings.

A circular road of some eighteen miles separates, to the seaward, the hotels, boarding houses and temporary accommodation of tourism from, to the landward side of the road, the homes of the permanent residents. It is the thoroughfare along which ramshackle buses, old lorries, walkers and cyclists mix and is thus the unmarked concrete separation zone between Rarotongans and their tourist guests. The only real reason for crossing that highway is either to climb the steep, narrow, twisting road to the hospital above, where the duty doctor in outpatients' may have seen as many as three cases that day, or to visit the Cook Islands Christian Church on a Sunday morning.]

Rarotonga was the most unexpected place for such a meeting between two such unlikely characters. Lush greenery, swaying palms, blue lagoons and swathes of sea-swept white coral sand formed the backdrop in as perfect a setting as may exist in reality and not merely created by the imagery and interpretive skill of a great atmospheric painter such as Gauguin.

Sadly, Tim Wilkins was not an artist – unless that word is applied as the second part of the recognised two-word euphemism for one who imbibes too freely of the demon drink!

Dorothy Moate, on the other hand, was one of that long and devout line of members of the Cook Islands Christian Church who have filled their beautiful chapel every Sunday morning at 10 o'clock for more than 150 years.

Oh no, that is not strictly correct. As the Cook Islands virtually straddle the International Date Line, it was not until some sixty years after the opening of the doors of the first church that the missionaries found out that they'd been holding Sunday worship on the wrong day.

To this day, 'though, the men still go to church in their best white suits and the ladies are proudly and carefully dressed in their summer frocks and costumes and ornate hats. They literally cram the building from floor to ceiling and fill the massive wooden balcony that runs around three sides of the interior. Dorothy was one of the two-thirds of Rarotongans who have always loyally supported the church with their voices and their presence. It is run on nonconformist lines by the London Missionary Society.

She had two main reasons for being present every week as well as a third, more practical one. As soon as the congregation departed, it was both her pleasure and her duty to scrub the steps with strong soap ready for the next service.

Two chief reasons for being there?

Firstly, through the religious fervour of her singing, to play her part in reassuring the Lord of her unquestioning support. It was an affirmation performed with passion, conviction and joy. Her second purpose was to help, through singing, to delight those all-important tourists who would, hopefully, show their appreciation of the pleasure absorbed through ear and eye in a practical way when the collection was taken. The Sunday service was by way of a marathon since much of it was said, sung or chanted in the native Cook Island Maori tongue as well as in English. It rarely ended in less than three hours. Tourists were strongly advised not to be tempted towards seeking the comfort and welcome coolness of a sheltered pew on the inside, not to mention the soothing breezes from huge slowly-revolving fans overhead, unless they were willing to stay until the final blessing!

Those who had taken such advice, but could not face so much worship and praise at one time, were welcomed to stand or sit on the lawns outside. As a continuous reminder of the constant powers of God both to move in a mysterious way as well as in giving and taking away, there was the tomb of Albert Henry (1907–81) to act as a salutary reminder of the wrath of God when challenged by the folly of man.

Albert reached the dizzy heights of becoming prime minister of the Cook Islands. He apparently made the cardinal mistake of putting his democratic faith in corruption rather than in God and came unstuck in 1978 when he used taxpayers' money to fly friendly voters back from New Zealand to support him. In the subsequent action, the High Court declared his victory to have been illegal and awarded the result to the main opposition party. He made history, later, when Queen Elizabeth stripped him of his knighthood – the first crooked politician to experience such public disgrace.

Sunday had always been a bad day for Tim Wilkins. He could not afford to buy drinks in hotels and quayside drinking haunts. Off licences, supermarkets and cheap local bars were closed for the day and members of the drinking fraternity gave him a wide berth at the best of times. His only hope lay in attending Sunday worship in the expectation of being invited back to someone's home afterwards.

He never looked untidy. Tim had the carefully prepared, perhaps over-presented, neatness of the professional alcoholic. Not for him the frayed cuffs, scuffed, unpolished shoes and greasy collars that are so often a giveaway.

Dorothy liked him. She was impressed by what she saw as his neatness, gentleness and sensitivity, as well as his seemingly obvious wish to respect and support the church and all it stood for. Their friendship grew and, as he looked up to that massive balcony week after week and saw the joyful radiance of her expression as she praised the Lord, he sometimes felt as if she was singing exclusively for him.

In a way he was right for, having shrewdly and accurately sized Tim up for what he was, she was indeed singing for the salvation of his soul and seeking to lay a magical musical pathway along which the repenting sinner could walk towards moral rectitude.

Such a one-way crusade could never succeed, she realised. Tim's redemption depended on much more than any personal rescue bid she might launch.

It happened after only a few weeks. One Sunday he arrived early for Sunday worship. His appearance and unsteadiness, his slurred speech and the overpowering smell of alcohol on his breath caused Dorothy to ignore the rule about not herself seeking to sit in judgment. Here was a sinner who was an embarrassment to the church, a violator of sanctity and decency and a stranger to respect.

The Lord had warned repeatedly that He would exact punishment upon unrepentant sinners. Dorothy, as a daughter of the Lord and a messenger of His will thought that immediate action from her was appropriate. She told Tim in no uncertain terms that since he had decided to take strong drink in the company of the devil, she would ask the minister to ban him. In the meantime her thoughts, feelings and prayers would be denied him.

When he suggested that she was being rather hard on him, she intoned: 'The ungodly shall not stand in the judgement, neither shall sinners in the congregation, of the righteous.'

In an uncharacteristic moment of attempted humility, he muttered some sort of an apology to her. She ignored it. Turning away, he stumbled against a corner of Sir Albert's tomb and mumbled a word she had never heard before. Indeed, had she heard it she would not have believed it could have fallen from his lips. However, an inner something told her it was a profanity.

It was an anagram of the initial letters of 'French Connection, UK!'

She opened her vast handbag and, producing two items, told him: 'The Lord will chastise your profanity on the Day of Judgment. But I will cleanse your foul forked tongue and filthy mouth here and now.'

And she did, with gusto, using the rough wire brush and bar of carbolic soap she always carried with her.

THE PROTECTOR

[It sometimes happens that a writer unintentionally strays into the world of puns.

Take this story, for instance, I have 'a confession to make.' I cannot find any justification in these politically correct times for having tried to amuse readers by my cheap and cynical portrayal of a two-sided priest who is, no doubt, the true spiritual and temporal father of his parishioners. Neither can there be any defence against charges of having used vulgar innuendo to help the plot along. And as for the defamation inferred against the integrity and sobriety of an upright maiden lady who is the third generation of her family to have dallied with the church organ....

So if I am prosecuted under some future law involving inciting religious hatred and ridicule, I will have to fall back on half a dozen character witnesses. They are all Roman catholics who have confessed (to me rather than at the confessional) to having found the story acceptable and funny.]

The day had started much as every other Tuesday had begun for the last fifteen years.

Michael wiped the last traces of toast and marmalade from his lips with his clean napkin and emptied his second mug of strong sweet tea.

As he placed the mug on the white nylon tablecloth, a door at the end of the room opened and, in total silence, other than with a nodded acknowledgment in her direction, the housekeeper, Mary Flanagan, gathered up the dishes and took them towards the door that separated Michael's room from the rest of the old building.

Two minutes later, as was the case every Tuesday (and all other days of the week except Sundays) she returned a few minutes later with a diary, a bundle of mail and a thick newspaper.

As soon as she had left the room, Michael changed the order of the pile so that the newspaper was on top, the diary in the middle and the letters underneath. 'This,' he thought to himself, 'is the real order of priorities.'

He made one other minor change. The thick newspaper, with its scribbled address '*The Presbytery*' was really two papers. On the outside, for dignity, decency and disguise, '*The Times of Ireland.*' Hidden discreetly inside was the real news he wanted to read, in the columns of '*Racing Post*'.

Michael, or to give him his full title, Canon Michael Dermot McCreevy, had come to the conclusion many years earlier that the role of a parish priest, with ample opportunities for a liberal personal interpretation of his duties and performance, was infinitely preferable to the (as he saw it) life of self-sacrificing masochism that might or might not earn him a bishopric later in his priesthood.

Michael was, by choice and instinct, an inveterate gambler. In the case of the Irish diocese in which he served, there was one bishop and almost one hundred clergy. Although, mathematically, the odds of attaining high office were technically fifty-fifty, the betting odds of his ever wearing the mitre were ninety-eight to one against.

It was working out such chances that had attracted him to horse-racing. There were, as he saw it, three justifications for indulging.

Firstly, it bonded him with the owners, trainers and punters who were important to the funding and attendances of his church, '*The Blessed Martyr of the Turf,*' as some folk irreverently called it. Secondly, he could not find any commandment which, however closely interpreted, actually banned gambling on horses. Thirdly, if he earned a good sum by using his judgment and mathematical skills, then he would not die in poverty and would therefore save the diocesan hardship fund from having to support him in his retirement.

Theologically, too, he could keep the proceeds. God would not bet if gambling was a sin so there was therefore nothing to render to God at the end of the day – other than thanks that his prayers had been answered in so specific a way. As Caesar was dead, there was nothing to be rendered in that direction either.

In any case he was not a gambler. He saw himself as an investor in a carefully assessed combination of the mixture of equine fitness and equestrian skill.

Having calculated the current status of his account at the local betting emporium of Messrs Paddy Power, he telephoned to indicate his passing fiscal interest and optimism in certain entrants 'coming under starter's orders' later that day.

He rather liked the phrase 'coming under starter's orders,' and decided it would make an excellent and appropriate sermon for use on the nearest Sunday to the Irish Grand National, perhaps linking it to the text 'Ye are my friends if ye do whatsoever I command you.'

There was, after all, only one great starter in the human race!

It was this thought sequence that turned a 'usual Tuesday morning' into something very different.

Normally, after sorting out his nags for the day (and the only other nags he ever really met were Sister Chastity and Sister Prudence on his dreaded weekly visits to the convent) he would read his mail. Today, while the inspiration for the racing sermon was fresh in his mind, he opened his diary to find the appropriate date.

He looked at the 'Today' page and saw, to his horror, that it had the word 'Music' underlined three times in red ink.

Of course, today was the second Tuesday in Lent when, without exception, a regular appointment had to take precedence over all else – his vital annual visit to call on Miss Bernadette O'Halloran.

By tradition the bishop of Raphoe visited Canon Michael's congregation in Mutterkenny, County Donegal, each year to celebrate Mass on Maundy Thursday. It was Michael's responsibility, ahead of this, to call on Bernadette, the organist at '*The Blessed Martyr*' on the second Tuesday in Lent to discuss the hymns for the visit and to listen to her suggestions for the processional music for the bishop.

It was one of the few regular duties he always enjoyed. Meeting Miss O'Halloran combined his personal pleasure and duty with her faith and innocence.

Bernadette, and everyone knew her as 'auntie,' was a pillar of the church. If anyone was sick, then she would call with her little covered basket bursting with appetising treats. No sooner had the angel of death crossed any threshold in the parish than auntie Bernadette was calling as the angel of hope and consolation able to light the shadows of grief with warmth and wisdom. A teenager with a problem would find, in her, tolerance and understanding dispensed with non-judgmental guidance.

No bird with a broken wing, or any lost or abandoned stray animal, would be better tended than in her tiny cottage with its ever-present smell of juicy apples. Indeed, apples symbolised her in every respect from the rosiness of her complexion to the delicate flavours and textures of her cooking.

If she had a vice then it could be argued that, in the same way that Father Michael saw it as his solemn duty to shore up the local horse-racing community, she believed she had a similar responsibility towards secretly sustaining the directors, shareholders, workers and sales figures of the town's whiskey distillery. It was a clandestine act known only to herself, the local off-licence and to the refuse workers who discreetly carried the empties away from her back door.

She had never married. Gossips hinted at a broken romance, a child surrendered to an orphanage, a womanly innocence that was too good to be true. She certainly possessed a worldliness that played hypocrite to her naivety.

She saw Michael long before he reached her front door. 'Blessed is he that cometh in the name of the Lord,' she said as she threw her arms around him in genuine warmth and with a crushing strength that belied her eighty-four years.

'And blessed are they that serve Him,' he replied before they joined in a common 'amen.'

She stood aside so that he could walk into the living room.

Although the priest might well have forgotten the day, Bernadette had been up early that morning to make some fresh apple tarts and a fruit cake ready for his visit.

'Make yourself at home, father. I'll be but a couple of minutes with the plates and a mug of tea.'

She went to the kitchen.

He strolled across the parlour to the old harmonium that had stood in the same corner since Bernadette's grandmother had become organist in the late 1870s. On it, as if already waiting for her recital and his approval, were several sheets of music.

But it was none of these that caused him surprise bordering on apoplexy and acute shock only a few short steps from cardiac arrest.

On the top of the instrument was a cut-glass Wexford bowl. In it – and he was not really sure if it was what he thought it was (or even if he ought to be thinking about the possibility of it being what it might be) – floated a small and almost transparent circular object in the most delicate shade of coral pink he had ever seen.

She returned carrying a tray with the food and two mugs on it.

Taking the bull by the horns, he said gravely: 'Bernadette, before we even talk about the music for the bishop's visit, is there anything you wish to tell me?'

'What about, father?'

'About, er, about sin,' he mumbled.

'And what sin do I have to talk about? We're all sinners of different degree in our minds, our behaviour and our bodies. But we know we can confess those sins and seek His forgiveness.'

131

'Bernadette, I have heard your confession many times, but you have never once mentioned any sins of the flesh to me.'

'I didn't want to bother you about small things like that. After all, it's only a tiny sin that I sometimes commit. Lots of people do it.'

The priest was horrified. 'Only a small sin of the flesh? It's far more serious than that, and you about to play for the bishop's visit.'

'All right, father, I will confess to the sin of gluttony. While I was in the kitchen preparing tea, I did eat a piece of cake and an extra apple tart. Surely I can be forgiven for that – even in Lent.'

'Bernadette, do you not realise that you have brought into your home the apparatus of the devil?'

'No, father, I've often heard you say that my fruit cake and little tarts are devilishly good, but I'm sure that's only a saying.'

She paused, thinking: 'Ah, father I see what you mean. Perhaps I shouldn't call them little tarts. Would "pies" be a better word?'

Canon Michael could not believe what he was hearing. 'What you are saying is profane, sacrilegious and untruthful. Do you have no shame, no remorse, do you not wish to confess and make penance.'

Despite her age, Bernadette was either a great actress or a brazen sinner totally beyond redemption, he decided.

'Bernadette, my daughter, how can you make so light of the sin of which you confess? Look at this... this... this obscenity. How do you explain it?'

He pulled her roughly across the room to the harmonium and pointed to the pink object floating serenely in the water in the cut-glass bowl.

'That?' she asked, 'What's wrong with it? It's wonderful. Using them regularly keeps me fit and healthy.'

'But where did you get it?'

'Well, father, a few months ago I was walking through Lovers' Dell and I found it in a little box wrapped up in foil. The box told me that if the contents were kept moist and placed on the organ they would prevent the spread of disease and infection.

'And they work. That was at the end of September and it's now February and I haven't had a cold all winter.'

132

THE SILLY STORY

[Silly stories need neither apology nor justification. If they did, then most of our tabloid newspapers would be out of business. After all, if the public didn't like silly stories, the red-tops wouldn't make such massive profits out of selling such material!]

It isn't easy to write a silly story.

The best way is, like most unsuccessful but desperate authors, to join a writers' group where you can experiment with weird mixtures of input ingredients (resembling those used by Macbeth's witches) and try to turn them into poems, stories or articles.

You know what I mean: one of the group describes a tennis ball and challenges other members to turn it into the depiction of a character or an event. The trouble is that it's the others who get the easy objects. I usually end up with a bar of soap, a button, an old ticket or something equally boring or useless. Then, while everyone else is trying to work their 'inspirational object' into a short story in the ten minutes allotted, I spend my time frustrated that, yet again, I didn't get something interesting like a photograph, a tap washer or an empty perfume bottle.

This summer evening the group gathering was different. The sinking sun poured a message of warmth and encouragement through the windows of the room in which we had met. It (the venue and not the evening sun) was part of the library. Something told me that, surrounded by the brilliance of published authors, I would be inspired.

My heart sank when I realised that the smarty pants who, on the basis of buggins' turn, had prepared the evening's task, and was approaching it with obvious sadistic enthusiasm.

In one plastic bag that had clearly seen better days as the last resort of some decomposing refrigerated food there were little bits of paper containing the names of women. Its companion was full of slips with men's names.

She then thrust a fan of coloured tourist pamphlets under our noses with the threateningly unspoken gesture of a conjurer who intends the victim to accept one without either thought or second choice.

Next she produced a tin. It was one of those long, narrow ones that used to be sold around Christmas, Coronations and Royal Weddings filled with cream crackers or chocolate biscuits. She offered it at a point well above eye-level and we were expected to plunge a hand into the unknown and withdraw one of the objects lurking within.

Knowing my luck, I approached this task gingerly fearful that my trembling and nervous fingers might engage with a grass snake, a dead baby rat or some other item of consummate repugnance.

I ended up with a large, flat unyielding object.

It was an oyster shell.

'Now,' she said in the tone of one who must be obeyed and not challenged, 'you each should have two names, the brochure for a summer tourist attraction and an object. You must bring them all together in a short story. You have ten minutes.'

The names gave me my first qualms. They were Mavis and Norman.

Bluntly, there's not much anyone can do to put flesh and blood on such boring bones as mental process attaches to the pairing of those names.

Why didn't I get Jo and Gervaise, or 'Tasha and Tristram? Now those are the sort of names around which modern short stories are woven. In fact if Tristram could be given a lilac shirt, a yellow tie, pink jeans and brogues and 'Tasha could be adorned in a prim little oatmeal twin set with matching accessories, they might even warrant a picture to go with a story in a women's magazine.

But rules are rules and Mavis and Norman they had to be. Of course, if the tourist attraction turned out to be a romantic location, I could perhaps arrange for them to meet 'Tasha and Tristram under the crystal waters of a waterfall. Mavis could fall in, Norman could fall to his death while trying to rescue her and, freed from their dreadful companions, 'Tasha and Tristram could have the sort of evening they – and my readers – would never forget.

But it was not to be.

The brochure was for Bonzo Sopwith's Flying Tigers Experience. Sadly, it just isn't feasible to drown people in an aircraft.

In any case, the object I'd drawn from the biscuit tin was a shell and not a waterfall.

I toyed with the idea of poisoning Norman with a contaminated oyster early in my story. Mavis, after a short period or mourning, could then embark on a bawdy and energetic aeronautical (with the emphasis on the 'naughty') escapade with Bonzo Sopwith.

There was, however, a simpler simple but more devious resolution.

At the last moment Mavis would fall ill from the after-effects of malaria and, rather than waste their pre-paid and non-refundable tickets for Bonzo's Flying Tigers Experience, Mavis and Norman would give them to their neighbours, Lisa and Noel.

Lisa and Noel were free spirits in every sense of the word. In fact the more the spirits flowed, the more experimental and less inhibited they freely became both in fantasy and reality.

Bonzo's brochure was an open-ended invitation to give everyone 'the chance to live out your dreams' on or in one or other of the Tiger Moth twin-winged aircraft operated by the Flying Tigers Experience. With more than 12,000 hours of experience as an instructor, he proudly claimed that no aerobatics were beyond the reach of his students.

Lisa and Noel had seen what is known as 'wing walking' at countless air shows and Bonzo assured them that aerobatic and acrobatic tricks were both simple and safe for anyone who followed simple rules of balance.

But Lisa and Noel's idea of a 'trick' wasn't exactly as conventional as merely standing on a wing. The correspondence columns of some of the adult magazines they read spoke of the exclusive Mile High club. They decided that, in fulfilment of Bonzo's claim to give everyone 'the chance to live out your dreams' they would qualify to join the club on the wing of a Tiger Moth while flying at 37,000 feet.

They took off and were soon confidently standing on the wings of the Tiger Moth and edging slowly towards one another. They embraced and slowly began to undress each other despite a wind-chill factor that suggested the wisdom dressing-up rather than the folly of stripping-down.

Bonzo's concentration was momentarily distracted by what was going on.

The aircraft lurched, spiralled out of control and crashed into a bog.

As the coroner put it so eloquently: 'This disaster was caused by ignorance rather than any other obvious technical or human factor. Air crash investigators recovered pieces of oyster shell from the wreckage and it is my conclusion, based upon that evidence, that the aviators mistakenly omitted to put Esso in the tank of their tiger in the hope that things would go well with Shell.'

THE PICNIC

[There's often a deep sigh in many a household as the closing credits roll on the latest adaptation of a novel by Jane Austen or the Bronte sisters. 'Why don't they write books like that now?' is usually the question. 'Why do we get revealing clothes, sex and violence in a plastic modern world when these novelists understood a genteel lifestyle dominated by honesty, integrity and by the rector who always had a young marriageable curate lurking in his vestry?

'And as for the lovely costumes, the safety and freedom of walks by the river bank, dogs that never fought each other or bit passersby. Why aren't people writing stories like that any more?'

I will tell you, dear reader in just nine words. 'Time, fashions, passions and moral values have moved on.' See if you can relate to this simple Then and Now.]

She may have been but thirteen years old, but Jodie Entwhistle knew beyond any possibility of contradiction that she would never read a book as tender, loving and understanding as *'Passion and Prudence'* by the great Victorian writer Josephine Morris.

How, Jodie wondered, could the spinster daughter of a country parson have known so much about the thoughts, needs and emotions of a woman? How, too, could Josephine Morris think and talk like a man when the characterisation so required? And how could a Victorian novelist know and write so protectively about the beauty of nature and the need for a commitment to the cause of environmental protection long before public conscience and awareness would become a national campaign and a personal duty?

But there it was – *'Passion and Prudence'* would be Jodie's favourite book of all time. She could even amaze her teachers by faultlessly quoting her favourite extract:

'They left the rectory in a small procession. At their head, searching, probing, sniffing sensing, the two black and white Springer spaniels, Roland and Benjamin.

'The Reverend Peregrine D'Argy-Fortescue, curate at St Olaf's church and Arabella Lovewell came next. Behind them swinging a picnic hamper and exchanging coy, romantic glances, were their chaperones for the evening. Mary, the pert and pretty sexton's daughter, was the junior housemaid at the rectory while her secret admirer, Richard, was in charge of the rector's stable of prize stallions.

'At the lych-gate Peregrine removed his black hat and, sweeping it low in a gesture of respect and courtesy, stood aside for Arabella to pass through first. She did so, acknowledging his gesture with a bob and a half curtsy. Aware that Mary and Richard were concentrating elsewhere and upon other matters, she added a brief yet privately coquettish smile towards the young curate.

'They strolled along the lane to the meadow. It seemed that Mother Nature herself had marshalled a vast panorama of sight and sound to greet them. The gentle humming of the bees and the endless chirping of grasshoppers supplemented the chorus of pigeons, cuckoos and song thrushes in a melodic orchestra of life. Tall fox gloves bowed to meet the upward-thrusting gold haze of buttercups while banks of daisies created a confetti carpet of such magnitude and delicacy as defied earthly belief and understanding. The contented bellowing of a tethered bull seemed to call upon the mooed responses of a dozen cows munching contentedly amidst the verdant meadow grasses.

'Mary and Richard set their pleasurable picnic burden on a grassy mound beneath a leafy oak tree. Peregrine beckoned to Arabella. Although it would have been improper had they touched one another, their minds and hearts were as one as he led her down to the river bank.

'Here the music was of a different manner. The rhythmic plop of a mayfly kissing the mirrored surface of the water; the occasional heavier splash as a salmon filled its belly, catching unawares some plump flying insect before swimming towards the next challenge of its life, the sparkling, thunderous restless water of the weir and the salmon leap.

'Two swans, their beaks glistening and with heads proudly erect, moved gracefully through the water as if in some timeless ballet set to the music of the bells of St. Olaf's peeling their joyful message across the distant sun-drenched fields.

'They walked back to a scene of transformation. Where their neat hamper had originally been set down, there was now a gingham cloth, napkins, china, polished cutlery, shining glassware. On plates were thinly-sliced salmon and cucumber sandwiches and tiny jars of potted shrimps. Even the crimson-skinned apples had been buffed to perfection. There were slices of game pie, sticks of asparagus, tiny quail's eggs in aspic, gooseberry and apple tarts and a greater variety of cakes and other confections than Arabella could recall having seen on any of her secret journeys to London to visit her father in the debtor's prison.

"Before we eat, my dear," the curate said, "let us despatch Mary and Richard to other duties. Perhaps they may care to exercise Roland and Benjamin awhile."

'With the excited giggles and laughter of children attending their first party, the servants made off towards the thick bushes that lined the lush green banks of the river.

'At last Peregrine and Arabella were alone. "Dearest Arabella," he said. "We have now courted one another for almost two years. I have something in mind and I must confess that I have already taken the appropriate steps to acquaint your dear mamma of my prospects and with a formal request for your hand ... ".'

'So saying, the curate removed the long-stemmed champagne glass from her slender fingers and held her left hand. It was white, delicate and as pure and doll-like as her own nature and character.

'I have about my person, indeed here in my pocket, something that, I pray, will give you joy and satisfaction forever.

'At this Arabella, not knowing what next to expect, swooned.'

Whenever she thought of that romantic river bank proposal, Jodie knew that it would have to be faithfully re-enacted to Josephine Morris' words were it to have any symbolic and lasting meaning for her when the right moment came.

And that was why, that sunny summer's evening, she and Rockie and his Pit bull terriers Coke and Cane were on their way to the romantic spot she'd discovered by the river bank.

The evening had got off to a bad start. Rockie was late. He was on probation and on electronically tagged curfew. He couldn't get out until the coast was clear. Then there'd been that awkward moment when the kissing gate wouldn't open. Some yobs had broken the hinge. Anyway, Rockie was more than a match for that. He lifted it off its brackets and chucked it over the hedge. At least he was brave, 'though, and walked through the opening first. Good thing he did, really, as there was a bull in the field. Big as a bloody tank it was. It snorted and pawed the ground.

Had Jodie paid a little more attention during rural affairs classes at school, she'd have seen that the bull was as sexually aroused as, it was already obvious, was Rockie.

The next field was rather like the meadow in the book – except it stank of cow-dung and liquid fertilisers. Coke and Cane didn't seem to bother as they'd found a decomposing rabbit chucked into the ditch. The probing of the dogs' noses upset a swarm of bluebottles and flies but – hey man, get alive, be real! – that's all part of the food chain, isn't it?

There was another smell, too. It didn't need a bloodhound to find that inconsiderate dog owners were responsible for that little intrusion.

At the bottom of the field, as in *'Passion and Prudence'* was a river. There were plenty of plops and splashes, but these were from the empty lager cans and breezer bottles that were being thrown down from the ancient bridge above for use as floating targets for a barrage of stones. There used to be a couple of swans there, but one had been shot by someone using a cross-bow. Its partner had drowned when it became entangled in fishing lines and couldn't be cut free in time from the supermarket trolley in which it was trapped.

Rockie and Jodie eventually found a small piece of rather smelly and dried-out grass for their picnic. They'd brought a bottle of cheap supermarket red wine, three tuna, gherkin, hot chilli and mayo wheat-germ-bread sandwiches and a giant economy-sized bag of crisps. Their main course would be the pepperoni, triple cheese and sizzled prawn pizza that Rockie was supposed to be delivering.

Their meal was eaten in silence. They were both thinking of exactly the same thing.

'Jodie, babe.'

'Yeah?'

'We've been going together four days so how about ... ?'

'I don't think it's right yet, Rockie. Let's give it another ten minutes.'

But Rockie was fast approaching his use-by moment. He was about to try the only suave means of seduction he'd ever learned – little realising how it would set off a chain reaction.

'I have in my pocket something that I know will give you lasting pleasure and satisfaction,' he said, 'just put your hand in my jeans. Don't be afraid. You'll remember tonight for the rest of your life.'

Jodie glanced down and could see a mysterious bulge deep in his pocket.

Fear and panic overwhelmed her. What could she do?

True to the spirit of the Brontes, Jane Austen and Josephine Morris, Jodie reacted as Arabella Lovewell and countless other women have done when their virtue was imperilled and since, in fact, tender romantic novels were first written.

She swooned.

She therefore did not see what happened next.

One of the dogs, Cane, decided it would be fun to chase one of the grazing cows which promptly ran off bellowing with fear. The bull, tiring of associating with the herd by remote control charged excitedly into the field with caution (and much else) exposed to the wind upon hearing the female bovine's cry.

Other than one of their number who rather contentedly lay back, thought of Jersey, and surrendered herself to the bull, the cows stampeded into the bushes from which there swiftly emerged no less than four courting couples. They were all confused and in varying states of disarrayed clothing and coitus interruptus.

Coke and Cane, seeing half naked humans in undignified and accelerating retreat, then enthusiastically took up a spirited chase across the meadows while the local gamekeeper, thinking that protected wildlife was in danger, fired a warning shot into the branches of a massive oak tree. His judgement at this time was somewhat impaired as he had spent much of the afternoon drinking rough cider in the bar of '*The Three Cocks.*' He staggered and was already falling backwards over a part-concealed tree root as the recoil of the gun threw him into the stinking duckweed and rubbish coating the stagnant water. Unfortunately the shot winged Rockie's probation officer who, when later interviewed by the police, explained that he had only climbed into the thick branches of the tree for a bird's eye view of the wildlife below. He stoutly denied being a peeping Tom and was later released with a formal caution for having acted in a manner likely to cause a breach of the peace.

And as for Rockie, well he was innocent of any improper thoughts or intentions. He'd merely put something in his pocket for Jodie – something he knew she wanted and would always enjoy and treasure – a battered second-hand paperback copy of '*Passion and Prudence.*'

THE LAST DROP

[Many of the world's best-known writers have based their stories on ideas or snatches of gossip they have overheard while listening to the conversations or scandal going on around them. It may have cost them the trust of an associate, or ruptured a friendship or two – but the end has always justified the means.

This seasonal yarn has been embellished by using a fragment of a short story written by Roald Dahl. This splinter, although not affecting the plot, tries to hold the narrative more tightly together with a sudden transfusion of the supernatural centred upon a picture.]

Had I even been a beggar I would have wished to be elsewhere. Yet I was not such a creature.

I was a hapless wayfarer seeking respite from the wintry storm that encased the very heart of the moor in an icy blinding grip of blizzard, snow drift and bog.

In truth I was exhausted and aware that, without shelter and sustenance, I would soon inevitably succumb to become yet another traveller who had foolishly and fatally challenged the savage elements of nature and might, for all I knew, be destined to lie unmissed and undiscovered to the end of time itself.

I know not what alerted me to its presence. Possibly it was the aromatic pathway of smoke wafting upwards and outwards from a log fire. Then, again, my eyes might have momentarily glimpsed lamps through that impenetrable blanket. Perhaps it was my sense of hearing that had detected the gentle creaking of rusty hinges swinging at the mercy of the wind.

On such possibilities or eliminations I will detain you no further since they are of little consequence to my account.

It came into view – a dark squat shape of greyness superimposed against the lighter shades of sweeping snow.

Possibly it was a farm building. In that blurred visibility it could have been almost anything. But, whatever it was it offered the chance of shelter.

No, as I neared that haven of hope and salvation I saw it was an inn. The creaking of those hinges drew my eyes to its quaint name, '*The Last Drop.*' I reflected for a moment upon the suitability of such a choice although, as I would learn later, even the name of that accursed place held a dark and sinister irony.

As I opened the door to enter, such conversation as had been in progress within was instantly ended. I was aware of eyes sitting at the rough-hewn oak tables. I say, 'eyes', for I could see nothing else of those who sat there. The combining of smoke and dim lamps with the broad-brimmed hats the customers wore made it impossible to see any faces properly. There was nothing to be seen between brim of hat and chin other than eyes. No mouths, no noses, no cheeks.

Nothing, just eyes.

I must now tell of the atmosphere inside that inhospitable place.

It may have been a combination of the wet clothing of those employed in farming or with cattle and horses, or the wool from their rough attire. This, coupled with the roaring log fire created a fierce and oppressive odorous stinking heat. Whatever it was, it issued forth an unpleasant stench of dirt, decay and decomposition.

The landlord of this dreadful place was as surly and curt as his customers.

Tiring of awaiting his attention, I called upon him for a flagon of wine.

He did not acknowledge my order and seemed unwilling to offer me even so much as a glance or nod of his head. I walked to the counter and repeated my request. This time he reacted but in such a way that I opined it would be incumbent upon myself to await the arrival of the wine from the cellar before taking it to my chosen table.

All the time those disembodied eyes watched my every move.

I was reminded of the visit of an earlier traveller, one John Burton, to a hostelry on another desolate part of the moor. He wrote of it thus: 'The moormen and the farmers came in; the great fire glowed like a furnace. The wind sobbed without, and piped in at the casement. The noise thus created, they said, was that of "souls on the wind" and was the chorus of the spirits of unbaptised babes wailing at the window-pane, seeing the fire within yet condemned to wander on the cold blast without.'

I approached the landlord and told him as much as I could recall of what I had read. He and the eyes seemed to accept the aptness of the description and I was then so incautious as to ask my host if it had, perhaps, occurred at his hostelry at some time in the past.

He ignored my attempt to converse although I sensed that the eyes were taking a new interest in me.

I tried a new avenue of discussion.

''*The Last Drop*' is an apt title for a public house,' I ventured.

'Why?' he countered.

'Because it indicates an endless service of unlimited hospitality and cheer,' I responded, regretting the obvious superficiality of my remark and my folly at having uttered it.

He sighed with the resignation of a wise man dealing with a fool.

'It has nothing to do with drink. Just look at those beams, those stout timbers across the fireplace and the hinges on the doors. They've all been brought here from the execution chamber at the old county prison. There's your "last drop," my friend.'

As if wishing to break off further conversation, he told me that the coach would arrive within the hour. I hoped that what he said was founded upon genuine concern for my welfare, but I rather gained the feeling that it was definitely his intention that I should take a seat upon it despite my obvious signs of exhaustion.

I questioned not that, although I had not once mentioned my intended destination, he had surmised that the coach would convey me thence. Whatever my exhaustion or my depleted ability to travel, the landlord had clearly decided it was time for me to go from the inn.

I mentally marvelled, instead, at the skill of any coachman and the surefootedness of his team to venture upon the exposed and treacherous highway on such a night. I could not convey any of this to the landlord as, having spoken, he turned his back upon me and busied himself with meaningless tasks to indicate that all communication between us was now at an end.

One of those wild sets of eyes summoned me across to join them.

'We've been over 'earin' that what Bob was tellin' 'e,' one of them said. 'We can see that you'm a man of some learnin' and us wondered if you do know what is th' first thing a 'angin' man don't see.'

The pairs of eyes chortled amongst themselves as if commencing some well-loved ritualistic local party game to be played with strangers.

'What is the first thing a hanging man doesn't see?' I repeated.

'Simple, the first thing he doesn't see at the moment of death will be the details of the faces of those in the crowd who have come to see him executed.'

146

The collection of eyes seemed disappointed to have been cheated so early of their prey. It would still be some time before the coach arrived. Perhaps they could carry their macabre game a little further.

'Here, mister, do 'e know as 'ow th' face is th' first thing as do go when you'm dead? Th' jaw, th' 'air an' th' eyes do stay, but th' face do go quick first.'

Their gallows humour failed either to entertain or amuse me.

I did not wish to discuss such rural beliefs or superstitions with them and turned my gaze to a picture upon the wall. It was of a small child throwing stones at a yacht upon a pond. I thought it was probably a little boy, but the detail was not clear.

''Ere, mister, I'll tell 'e somethin' true 'bout that picture,' one of that congregation of eyes said.

'Th' last landlord but one 'ad it up on 'is wall. 'T'were 'is prized ownin'. One day 'is little daughter went missin'. Everybody scoured the moors but there were no sign o' th' maid. Three weeks later, well after the search were called off, th' landlord just 'appened to look close at th' picture and 'e see'd that th' boy in it'd changed to a faceless girl wearin' the same clothes as what 'th' little maid went off in.

'No mortal 'and could've changed th' picture.

''E went over Drackly Pool and there 'e did find th' earthly remains o' th' little tacker in th' reeds with all 'er face gone. Like we all do agree 'ere, th' face do go first for to go on to someone else while it's still fresh.'

I was alarmed as much by what I had heard as by the silence that followed. I was so upset that I ordered a tankard of beer and moved to a table nearer the door in order that I would not miss the coach as it drew nigh on its journey onwards to whatever destination lay ahead in the unyielding savage ferocity of that night.

At last it arrived. It may have been the mixture of cheap wine and rancid beer, but as I stood to wrap my cloak around me, I was aware that my breathing had become laboured; my chest felt as if it were being crushed. There was an increasing feeling of pain in my arm. My legs were giving way.

I fell to the floor. The bearer of one of those pairs of eyes stooped over me as if to pick me up and carry me out to the coach.

I saw to my horror that he was already wearing my face.

147